Love,

Technically Speaking

Flaps, Sazzle Machine, Unicorn Poops & Moody Maggie –

Thank you for being my reasons to stay, and even though we parted,

here's to the ending we should have had.

Love, Technically Speaking

Chapter ONE

Josie

"Today is THE DAY!" A voice yelled excitedly from my phone, which was precariously balanced on the edge of the sink I was washing in. I hummed in agreement, mouth foaming with toothpaste and, catching sight of a forehead line that I was sure hadn't been there yesterday, proceeded to frown harder at myself in the mirror and poke at my face. The toothbrush stuck out across my cheek, eyes watering from the minty-fresh extra strong flavour. "Did you get rid of Glenda?"

I spat the toothpaste into the sink, turned the tap on to wash it down and began to examine my chin, confirming the absence of a regular random hair that we had affectionately named. "She's gone."

"And Glynis?" Another glance underneath at where her 'twin' often appeared.

"Her too." There was a chuckle from the phone, and I smiled at the handset as I wiped my mouth and shut the tap off; trust Rosie to consider my random chin hairs worth a discussion on what promised to be a big morning for me. I inspected my face in the mirror once more. I had been growing my hair for a few months now, and the brunette waves had finally reached my shoulders. I used my washcloth to wipe my mouth before throwing it into the laundry bin in the corner of the bathroom.

There was a sudden drilling noise coming from my phone as I picked it up and carried it out of the bathroom, "What on earth is going on over there?"

"Hang on!" There was a yell, a few bangs and scuffles and the drilling noise got suddenly quieter as a door clicked shut. "It's Mike. You need to come save me." Rosie pleaded with me down the phone.

I laughed as I pulled out a cold pain au chocolat, and glanced at the phone again, "Why? What is he doing now?"

"It's the blender. He's making smoothies with fruit I don't even like! If it isn't this or overnight oats, he's forcing avocado." There was a noise, and I pictured her shuddering in disgust.

"Sounds delicious, he can come and make me some!" Rosie was the pickiest eater and despite having regularly heard her tell our patients about good food to eat, she secretly consumed inordinate amounts of junk. "But why the sudden need to eat healthy breakfast?"

"Oh, *he* doesn't eat it. He's making me eat it to make sure the baby is healthy. I *told* him that having a breakfast biscuit won't harm and I *did* say that if my body says I need to have pickled onions and chocolate spread on toast, I should listen to it!" There was a pause on the line, and she began to whisper urgently, "He doesn't know I've been tipping the juice out the window when he wasn't looking, but now I've discovered algae growing down the wall outside!"

I laughed and shook my head. My boss and best friend was on maternity leave and much to her horror, she had just become my ex-boss and today was my first day in a new job.

"Anyway, I'll figure that out later. What are you wearing? Have you got stationery, notepad? Lunch? Drink? Oh, you haven't forgotten the special mug, have you?"

"You mean the one with the photo of us shaking bottles of amoxicillin on it? I have it – but the story behind the photo is not something I'm willing to share with people I only just met!" There was a giggle down the line and seeing the time, I grabbed my things, gave Astrophe a quick goodbye stroke and locked the front door. "I'm getting in the car now."

"Look, you're going to smash it. Go show them what pharmacy technicians are made of, right? You know your stuff and you're amazing. Ok and Jos, one last thing. I don't care if every single person in that GP practice is bloody awesome, don't you dare replace me as your best friend."

I grimaced as I started the engine and shook my head. "Not possible – I don't think I could find a pharmacist that drives me as mad as you do! Now go drink the smoothie!"

"I've got chocolate raisins hidden in my dressing gown pocket – don't tell him! Love you!" The phone clicked off and I pulled the car away from the drive, sighing with nerves. I'd worked in community pharmacy for so long, it seemed absurd to move into a new role, and into a completely different sector! From what I remembered of the surgery the rooms were very unfriendly and clinical, but the lady showing me round had seemed nice. When I'd been shown the reception room, the cluster of faces had all looked welcoming, if not a tad overwhelming, and the pharmacy office had seemed cosy.

The decision to move wasn't one I'd taken lightly but I just felt like I needed the change. My team had been my family and though I wasn't unhappy, I needed something to stretch me a little bit, a fresh challenge. Or at least that's what the confident side of me had said in my interview. I had been stalled in my working life and in my home life and admitting to myself that it was time for a fresh scene had taken me by surprise. I lived to work, had next to no social life anymore, and I did the same thing every day. I wanted to break out of the rut and not only think outside the box but live outside it too. My last day in the pharmacy had been overwhelming and I had sobbed as though it wasn't just down the road, and I couldn't pop in whenever I fancied.

As I pulled up to some traffic lights, my mind wandered back to a few weeks prior when I'd called into the practice for my interview. A kind-faced lady had welcomed me in the waiting room after the woman on reception had asked me to take a seat. Anne had taken the opportunity to show me around and introduce me to two of the doctors.

Both had been unsmiling, not unkindly, just very keen to proceed with questioning about my experiences. I was honest though, I had no experience in general practice and despite having led various healthy living community schemes and having been married to my job for several years, I really didn't have much to show for my work.

I hadn't expected to be offered the job in all honesty and when I left the practice, said goodbye to Anne and nodded to the lady on reception, I had pulled out my phone and told Rosie she should probably expect to return to business as usual after mat leave. It was the phone call the following day that had shocked me, "When can you start?"

I was shaken from my thoughts by an urgently beeping horn; the traffic lights had turned green, and my lack of movement had clearly annoyed the driver of the car behind. I set off, frowning in the mirror at the car driving too close to my rear. *Does he want to sit in my back seat?* I could see that the driver was shaking his head and I cursed and waved my hand to apologise, but he pulled into the lane next to me and raced past.

It didn't take long before I caught him up though, as a red at the next set of traffic lights had us lined up neck and neck. I pulled up next to a very sleek, black, and expensive looking Lexus and turned to look inside. The tinted window was already half-open revealing a tousled-blonde and frowning man, whose jaw line could have cut me in two. He looked directly into my eyes with a dark expression that hit me hard. My stomach spasmed. Wow, if looks could kill I'd have needed a coroner.

"Driving *requires concentration*!" He stated loudly through his window and sneered at me as the window began to close, and I took a deep intake of breath, feeling the anger rise inside. It was as though a match had been lit in the pit of my stomach - what a jerk! Nobody sneered at me, Lexus or no Lexus! Noticing the lights were about to change, I lifted my middle finger through the window in his direction and stomped on the accelerator at the same time, wheels spinning against the tarmac, not even waiting for a response. *Requires concentration? He could do one.*

"Come on, Terry!" I urged my little car forward, pulling away from the traffic lights faster than Mr Lexus. "Hah! So long, sucker!" Mentally high fiving myself, I raced up the road. I found impatient people irritating and unforgiving people, hard to get on with. Quick to judge, and easy-to-snap types of personality had always been the most challenging, perhaps because I had always been an accommodating person and much to my own dismay, a people pleaser. Mr Lexus was clearly one of those snotty, snobby kind of men who saw to it that people paid for their mistakes, and I huffed in annoyance thinking of his sneer.

I turned left into the street towards the practice and abandoned all thoughts of the other car, overcome by a sudden wave of nerves. The brick building came into view: frosted glass windows, queue of rather miserable looking patients outside the front of the door and a sign indicating the car park to the rear of the building. It might not look it but, this was it: my new start.

I pulled round the back and into a space, turned off the engine and quickly texted Rosie to say that I had arrived, before swinging my legs out of the car. I was just pulling my brand-new work bag out of the boot when I suddenly spotted a black Lexus passing behind me. I paused for a panicked second, thinking back to the traffic lights.

The car pulled in smoothly a few spaces down, in front of which I spotted the sign inscribed 'Doctor' heading up the space and my heart sank as I recognised the blonde locks of a Mr, no...clearly a Dr Lexus climbing out.

"Crap!" I whispered to myself and ducked next to my car, "Well done, Josie." I cursed myself and scurried inside before he spotted me. Of all the people this could happen to, it would be me. My heart sank a little as I approached the desk, and I hoped that whoever he was, he would not recognise me or my middle finger.

"Hello, I'm the new pharmacy technician!" I said, rather too cheerily, over the counter to the same receptionist who I remembered from a few weeks prior. She glanced up curiously and smiled as she stood.

"I'm Debbie, nice to meet you, do come through." She led me through a door I hadn't spotted and straight to Anne's office which I remembered from last time. "You've met Anne our practice manager?"

"Thanks, yes." I smiled and stepped inside, desperately hoping that Dr Lexus wasn't about to come in.

"Welcome! Gosh, it only seems two minutes since your interview. I've got a list of documents for you to fill in and read, and then we can start on your induction. How did you find the journey?" She handed me a pile of documents and ushered me into a seat near the table in her office. Short in stature and with long, dark wispy hair, Anne commanded an air of authority which far superseded her height. She seemed kind, though I felt as though there could be a strictness in her if I should be so deserving.

"It was fine, only took me 15 minutes." I sat at the table to begin filling the forms in and reading various documents as Anne returned to her desk. The information was dull and the task truly boring.

"Josie, this is Dr Ambrose." I broke away from reading to smile and shake his hand. He was a large chap, with a beaming smile detracting from his rotund belly. "And this is Dr Cook and Dr Li."

Dr Cook was an unpleasant looking man, not in his appearance per se, but his apparent disdain for my existence. Compared with a jovial welcome from Dr Li, Dr Cook's welcome was positively frosty. I smiled and nodded anyway, though my heart sank a little. I felt like he might be one to watch.

Before I knew it, I'd been broken off from reading more than six times and I had already forgotten most of the names of the various members of staff that had wandered into Anne's office. It seemed to be the central hub for activity, and when one doctor left, a nurse replaced her, followed not long after by a receptionist and a member of admin. I had reached the point of just nodding and smiling as each one approached, and I think Anne eventually decided she had introduced me to enough people for the moment, and a period of silence ensued.

I was just getting to reading the social media policy – juicy stuff – when I heard Anne call me, her distant voice seeming to pull me from my reading-induced reverie "Josie?"

I looked up to discover she was looking at me rather expectantly, as if she had already needed to repeat herself. "Oh, I'm sorry, I was glued to the paperwork!"

"That's ok, just one more introduction for this morning." She smiled and gestured to the door. "This is Dr Reeve, our lead GP for the pharmacy team." I glanced up to discover Dr Lexus himself, leaning in the doorway and as our eyes met, there was a spark of recognition and his signature sneer appeared. Oh, he was gorgeous, sneer or not, and I was momentarily stunned with a mixture of awe and embarrassment. His suit fit him like a glove, his hair naturally coiffed in a style that made my fingers itch to trawl through it, and the intensity of his stare had my toes curling in my newly purchased work shoes.

"Ah. Ms. Toyota." He said in a slow, deep voice. I swallowed a laugh nervously, cringing at the awkwardness of the encounter and yet irritated, nonetheless. It was typical that I would somehow have found myself a boss that I had managed to offend before I had even stepped foot in the building.

"It's Josie, nice to meet you." *Should I apologise for giving him the finger?* "About the er-" I began.

"I'm rather busy so must go, if you'd been listening before, you'd have heard I have a meeting to attend." *Oh really?* I raised my eyebrows as my mouth fell open in surprise. I blinked stupidly at him while there was a pause; his eyes burned into mine, as if challenging me for a response, my embarrassment transformed into stubborn defiance, and I frowned.

"Nick-" Anne began but I spoke up quickly, my brain scrambling for a response.

"That's ok Dr Reeve. Sorry I missed it; I always forget how much reading *requires concentration.*" I smiled broadly, casually dripping sarcasm, and taking great care to emphasise his words back to him.

"Lovely to meet you." A smug smile punctuated my response and there was another pause.

He gave me a fleeting frown before striding out of the office and I turned to look at Anne. She said lightly, "Don't worry about him Josie; it takes time to get to know him."

I smiled faintly and pulled open the absence policy. I'm not sure I wanted to get to know the impatient, sneering Dr Reeve with his lousy Lexus. Terry the Toyota beat its expensive bodywork with character any day, I told myself and nodded, harrumphing in annoyance. Anne looked up at me curiously and I smiled sweetly and returned to my work with a shake of the head and a small sigh; what a bloody start to a new job.

Chapter TWO

Josie

"I'm not kidding, Rosie. I gave my new boss the middle finger." I hissed down the phone from the toilet cubicle I'd hidden in. There was a shout of laughter and a muffling of the phone.

"Well Jos, there are better ways to make a good impression." Mike said, and I could still hear Rosie laughing in the background.

"Guys I'm serious – what do I do?" I hadn't spotted Dr Lexus for the rest of the morning and once I'd finished the paperwork, Anne had sent me to have a break and a coffee. I'd found a bathroom after wandering up a stairwell and passing a row of closed doors.

"Do nothing! Just carry on like nothing happened and he will soon forget." Mike said. I was standing in the cubicle and picking at the tatty sign tacked to the door. *'Treat 'em mean, keep 'em clean',* it said above a cartoon image of a person looking far too excited to be holding a toilet brush.

"How could I possibly be such a moron?" There was a click in the cubicle next to me and I froze. Someone else was in the bathroom and they were sure to have heard me. "I'll call you later!" I quickly clicked the phone off and opened the door to see the reflection of a woman smiling back at me. I smiled awkwardly as I approached the sink to wash my hands in. Her hair was striking: blonde fading into pink waves, and she had a nose piercing glinting in the light.

"You're not the new technician, are you?" she said as she turned her tap off.

"I'm guilty of that yeah, I'm Josie." I smiled as I soaped my hands up. She grinned even wider and reached for some paper towels.

"Oh great! I'm Talia! I work in prescription clerking!" She did a little jump with excitement and her hair bounced with her too. I liked her already. "I'm so sorry darls, but I couldn't help but overhear your conversation! Which boss did you give the middle finger?" She looked at me with a mischievous grin and my face dropped into a look of horror.

"Oh, you didn't!" I moaned, shook my hands over the sink and reached across her for paper towels. She nodded and waited expectantly. "On my way here, there was a car that drove a bit too close to me and we ended up next to each other at some lights. I might have given the driver the middle finger only to realise that it was one of the doctors here when I pulled up." I felt the heat flood my cheeks as she burst into giggles and threw her paper towel into the bin. I'd have said she was late twenties, a little younger than me, and she just seemed so pleasant. Her high-waisted black trousers cut her work blouse nicely and she had these cute boots on which made her look taller than me.

"That is so funny! Which doctor? Has he realised it's you?" She said as she opened the door for us both.

"Dr Reeve." She gasped in horror and burst into fresh giggles as I followed her down the corridor, her boots clacking against the lino flooring.

"Of all the GPs you could have done that to! Wow, you're a legend. He's a tough nut to crack that one." She said as I scuttled along behind. I had serious hair envy; the pink was beautiful.

"He is?"

"Yeah, he doesn't say a lot which is usually a good thing. When he does speak, you know you've done something wrong." She led me down a second corridor to a door, "Do you want to come and meet the team?"

"Sure, you don't think Anne will mind?" I said hesitantly, conscious my coffee break was probably more than over.

"She was probably bringing you this way, anyway." She tapped a code into the keypad on the door and there was a brief bleep and the door swung open to the sound of laughter. A large rectangular room filled with desks and computers spread out before me and three faces suddenly turned to the door.

"Ladies... this is Josie our new technician!" There was a pause as I smiled awkwardly and gave a little wave.

"Hi!" I felt my face burst into flame as I took in each of their faces from behind their monitors. There was a sudden chorus of 'hello!'

"We're a bit of an odd bunch really," A woman with brown hair stood and came to embrace me in a hug.

"Speak for yourself, I'm Tina." There was a laugh as I took a good look at her. She was blonde, shorter than me and wearing the same blouse as Talia. "I do the same job as Talia over there. And this oddball here is Rachel." She nodded backwards to the woman with brown hair.

"And that's Holly!" Talia pointed to a darker haired woman who was still talking on the phone, "Have a look around, I'll just send Anne a message so she knows where you are." They sat at their desks and in the time it took for me to notice an empty desk between Talia and Rachel, Tina had already answered another call.

There were two big whiteboards on the far wall, lists of what looked to be names of care homes and dates next to them. There were doctor names up there as well, I felt a pang of unease when I saw Dr

Reeve's name, and telephone numbers for various departments scrawled to cover every inch of the boards. On the near side wall there were posters for local services and to the side was a window, which upon closer inspection overlooked a courtyard. The room was suddenly full of chatter as each member of the team spoke on their own separate telephone call.

"How are you getting on?"

"-listed side effect."

"It was issued yesterday-"

"...is it itching?"

I observed them for a short time, fascinated by the things they discussed, but then Talia pulled open her drawer as she hung up on her call and pulled out what looked to be a snack bar. She got up and grabbed a mug from each of the girls' desks and plonked them onto a tray.

"Do you want a tea?" She asked.

"Coffee if you don't mind, please. Is this going to be my desk?" I nodded to the empty space, and she beamed.

"Yes! We couldn't wait for you to start. If you come with me downstairs to the kettle, you can grab your things." I followed her out. "Oh, do you have a mug?"

"Downstairs." Trailing behind as she clicked her boot heels down the steps and balanced the tray of mugs, I couldn't help but feel comfortable. It was almost as if today wasn't my first day; I quite liked it really.

"So, you're new to working in general practice?" She asked me as I held open the door for her at the bottom of the stairs.

"Yes, community pharmacy was my last role. I loved it but fancied a change." She led me past the offices to a little kitchenette. "So are Rachel and Holly pharmacists?"

"Rachel is a technician; Holly is a pharmacist. Do you want to grab your mug?" I nodded and turned back towards where we had passed Anne's office. Her door was open still and she was sitting with her desk phone tucked into the crook of her neck. I tapped lightly on her door and when she looked at me, I pointed to my bag. She nodded and smiled, and I pulled out the mug that Rosie had given me. On one side there were our beaming faces smushed up next to each other and on the other, we were both shaking bottles of amoxicillin with cross-eyed expressions – don't ask - it's a story for another time. I turned to leave and stepped out of Anne's office, and walked straight into a wall of hard chest.

"Umpf-" My mug dropped.

"Looks like you pay as much attention to where you're walking as you do to traffic lights, Toyota." Dr Reeve stepped back to allow me to glance at his face and I was momentarily dazzled by the smell of his aftershave. It was nice. Manly. But his face was still sneering, and I apparently was still staring at him.

"Sorry, Dr Reeve" I stepped out of his way and started to walk towards the kitchenette in a daze.

"Toyota?" I turned back to him. "I'd ask if this was yours, but it has your face all over it." He held out the mug I'd dropped, thankfully intact, and I felt myself turn a shade of pink as I took it from him.

"Thank you." I turned to walk away and then suddenly, angry at still being called Toyota, turned back to him. "Dr Reeve?"

"Yes?" His head snapped back around.

"I'm Josie." He raised his eyebrows and smirked. *Arse.* I turned back to the kitchenette and passed my mug to Talia, who rinsed it and tipped in some coffee granules.

"Why is Dr Reeve like that?" I said.

"An arse?" Talia whispered and smiled as I nodded. "He's our training lead - you wouldn't think so, would you? But honest, once you're trained by him, you'll be fine. We have our training afternoon on

Wednesday this week and I think he's leading. Come on, grab your bag, we will get you settled in."

The rest of the day was hectic, and I found myself learning door codes, login details, passwords, and the intricacies of the patient record system. I spent a lot of time asking the girls questions and listening to their conversations. Being a pharmacy technician in a general practice was going to be very different to life in community pharmacy. I was going to be able to support patients in managing their medicines in a whole new way, and suddenly the excitement at being a part of the team was overwhelming.

"How was your first day?" Anne asked me as I poked my head around the door at 5pm, bag slung across my shoulder.

"It was great, and the team are so friendly!" I said, grinning, "There's a lot to learn but that's why I'm here."

"Well, you certainly seem to have made a good impression on the team; we are looking forward to getting to know you. See you tomorrow, Josie."

I smiled and turned to leave, waving at the ladies in reception who I'd met briefly earlier, and set off down the back corridor that I'd been told staff tend to use. At the end, there was a door that I pushed but it wouldn't budge. I pushed again, and again but harder. *Was I stuck?* I rattled the door handle and pressed against the glass in frustration when there was a sudden click and beep.

"There's a release button." I turned sharply, winced at a sudden pain in my neck and discovered Dr Reeve leaning against the wall next to the door, eyebrows raised in amusement, and fingers on said release button.

"Ah. Yes. Thank you." I flushed and grabbed the handle.

"Just for the record," He said and held the door before I could open it, "A Toyota would never pull off quicker than a Lexus."

I swallowed a laugh and looked him in the eye. "Well, I guess that depends on who's driving." And with my own little smirk, I pulled the door free of his grasp and strode out into the cold air.

Chapter THREE

Josie

"Hello, it's Josie, how can I help?" I heard myself say on my very first call with a patient. I listened intently to them and smiled to myself, thrilled to be finally having a go with talking to people again.

"It...it's my inhaler.... I can't seem to get it going," There was a voice down the phone, with audible wheezing.

"Can I take your name first please and date of birth?" Rachel sat next to me, ready for if I needed anything and I fumbled a little with clicking the search function. Locating the patient on the system, I began asking questions and it occurred to me that I felt the lady at the end of the phone needed to be seen in person. "Bear with me while I just put you on hold, Mrs Mason. Rachel, how do I go about seeing this lady in the practice? She wants to know what she's doing with her new inhaler."

"Well, there are a few options. We could ask her to discuss it with her community pharmacy, she could come in and discuss it with one of us or we could see if Holly can speak to her as part of her med review clinic. Can you see if she's been seen recently?" She leaned over and showed me how to search the records and after another chat with the patient, we made a plan.

"How was that?" Rachel smiled kindly, and I nodded in relief.

"Good – I'll get there!" I spent much of Tuesday morning getting to grips with the computer system. Interacting with the patient record was a challenge as there were so many different functions and buttons on the screen. A sudden box appeared in the corner of my screen: *'Miss Tina Wright 10:08: Want a coffee?'*

"Instant messaging?" I turned incredulously to Tina who was two desks away.

"Yes – you can send a message to anyone logged on. The message will appear on their screen just like mine did on yours. Send me a reply." She turned back to her screen while I clicked on the reply button and typed a response.

"Two sugars!" She stood, after reading my reply, and grabbed the mugs from our desks, "We are all sweetener-takers here."

"I need sweetening up…" I grinned as she opened the door to leave. For only my second day in the practice, I already felt like one of the team. Holly, our pharmacist, had introduced herself and assured me she was always there for support, but she had been absent in clinic for much of the morning. Rachel, my fellow tech was going to be a great friend, I could feel it already. Talia and Tina were incredible too, their continuous supply of snacks and drinks was welcomed but I had concerns for the future of my waistline.

"What was your last job like, Josie?" Talia enquired when she hung up her call. I paused, my hand in mid-air about to pick the telephone up and turned to her.

"It was great. My manager was my best friend, and we were the perfect team." I smiled as I thought of my time with Rosie.

"Why did you come here, then?" She looked genuinely curious, and Rachel had finished her conversation and was now listening intently.

"Sometimes you just need a change of scene. I loved my job, but I felt stalled. I felt like I had more to offer. And even though I know I could have done more training, I just felt like I needed a change in direction. Am I making sense?" I smiled.

"Yeah, that's fair enough! You have to do what makes you happy, don't you?"

Rachel leaned in, "You're welcome here anytime. I need to give you my number as well." She reached for a pen and paper.

"Thanks. I'm just not sure I'm up to the job if I'm being honest. I'm a bit nervous that I'll make a mess of things and regret the change." And as soon as the words left my mouth, I felt the knot of anxiety in my chest twist. It almost felt like I'd been denying the feeling but now I'd acknowledged it, it felt consuming. Community pharmacy had been my home, it had been safe. I knew my job, my colleagues, and my patients inside out. I'd gone from being hugely competent to suddenly completely incompetent and like a fish suffocating out of water. I was honestly quite terrified. What if I really, genuinely sucked at this job and found myself having to leave? Would Rosie take me back? And would I want to go back and admit my failure to the patients who had wished me well? I shuddered involuntarily and Rachel put her hand on my arm, a look of concern on her face.

"Hey, it's ok. We all felt like that, and we all have your back. It really is scary and to be honest, sometimes there will be unpleasant moments. But that's what we are here for."

"Are we going to a funeral?" Tina said as she barged through the door, balancing mugs on a tray. We all looked at her in shock. "The glum faces!"

I giggled as Talia chirped up, "No... it's just our Josie doubting herself."

"A DEBBIE DOUBTER?!" Tina yelled. "Not a chance. We don't doubt our abilities in here, Jos." *Our Josie.* My heart swelled as I realised just how much I felt like I fitted in already.

"She's right, you know." Holly followed her in, carrying her own mug. "It's so easy to think less of yourself when you're definitely capable of more. I always doubt myself, but we bolster each other in this team."

"We sure do." Rachel said kindly, and then there was a sudden burst of calls on two of the phones. I pulled my attention back to the screen and started looking down the pharmacy team inbox that was littered with tasks attributed to patients by their names. I clicked on one, *'This patient wants to know why her medicines are all out of sync'* and then another, *'this lady has been discharged with no medication – discharge in record'* and then another, *'this patient doesn't understand how to take her medication – can you help?'.*

"Josie, there's a task on there I feel would be a good one for you – the patient needs help understanding the timings of medicines as the discharge has changed some of them. Do you see it? Want to give it a go?" Holly pointed me to the right task, and I pulled up the information and got on with calling the patient. It never failed to amaze me how when people were moved in and out of hospital, information about medicines got lost in translation.

"Well, they've sent me home and not given me any bisoprolol!" Mrs Cross said on the telephone.

"You don't need to take that anymore Mrs Cross, would you like me to go through the list of medicines you're down to take now and we can chat about them?" I asked her politely.

"Yes, lovey but speak up!" It was a lengthy conversation, but I couldn't help but feel like I'd made a difference to her in some small way. I spent much of the morning picking out things I felt I could do, asking questions all the time and occasionally having to put patients on hold while I asked about where to find bits of information.

"Lunch?" Talia asked when I hung up the phone to my last patient.

"I thought you'd never ask." I grabbed my bag and trotted after her clacking heels.

"What's on the menu?" she asked, pulling a soup out of the fridge in the staffroom and passing me my lunchbox.

"Last night's lasagne reheated," I suddenly spotted an influx of people through the door. There were a number of nurses and healthcare assistants – their uniform made it obvious – and one or two suited people that suggested they might be GPs. I suddenly got that anxious feeling again – incredibly self-conscious and very much feeling like I stuck out like a sore thumb as the new girl.

"Quick, grab the microwave before anyone else jumps in," Talia held the microwave door open for me once she removed her soup. "What's wrong?" She eyed me, concerned.

"Uh…erm… I just feel a bit nervous because I don't know anyone." I occupied myself with working out how to use the microwave while she made us coffee.

"Don't worry – you'll soon get to know everyone, darls." It was at that point that I spotted Dr Reeve striding into the now very busy staffroom. Nurses were sitting around a table opening packed lunches, the smell of salads and sauces assaulted my nose, and there was a queue forming behind me for the microwave.

"Ah, holding up the queue again I see, Toyota." Dr Reeve muttered as he leaned above my head to get into the cupboard – he didn't even stop to look at me. The delicious smell of aftershave hit me again, this time coupled with a clean washing powder fragrance from his very neatly pressed blue shirt.

"I suppose I am." I said and stuck my chin out in defiance. "It isn't against the law to heat up lunch, is it?"

"No but it's rather annoying when there's a queue for the microwave and the person cooking their food is ignoring the beeping of a finished meal..." I paused and glanced at the microwave to discover it was, in fact, beeping incessantly to tell me my food was cooked. I glanced up to where Dr Reeve was now staring straight into my eyes with a look of triumph and frowned.

"Well...thanks" I pulled my box of lasagne from the microwave and headed to a table in the corner where Talia was sitting, feeling his eyes burning into my back as I crossed the room.

"What happened? Dr Reeve is staring at you." She raised an eyebrow before sipping her soup as I sat down.

"I really got his back up with the middle finger incident yesterday morning." I said, rather glumly.

"Ha! I keep forgetting about that. Well, he was smiling anyway. Uh... we were talking about work," I frowned as she hissed and shuffled slightly and looked down at her soup and then realised the change of topic was because Dr Reeve himself had approached the table where we were sitting. "Hi, Dr Reeve!"

"Talia. It is my training session tomorrow, hoping I'll have a full team there – will you be joining us?" He looked at me.

"I presume so, yeah." I nodded

"Good. Don't get distracted and be late, there's a lot to get through." He raised his eyebrows at me and then left; Talia's mouth fell open once he was out of earshot and through the door, and she chuckled.

"Wow." I said, "I really haven't made a good impression, have I?"

"Actually, I'd say you have." She shifted in her seat, and I began to poke at my lasagne while I waited for her to have another spoonful of soup. "That's the first time Dr Reeve has ever acknowledged me outside of the training room. And he only spoke to me to make a point to you."

"And your point is?" I said and shovelled in a mouthful.

"Well – you've entertained him and he's quite enjoying making you squirm." She said, quite matter-of-factly and spooned in more soup. My mouth was full and all I could do was manage a roll of the eyes.

I swallowed. "Fantastic." We ate in amicable silence. Talia pulled out her phone and began tapping away while I pondered the strange Dr Lexus. At some point he would get bored of playing whatever game he was playing with me, for now I just had to keep out of trouble.

"So, what do these training sessions usually involve?" I said as we left the staffroom and walked more slowly back to the office

"Well, usually we have a different GP run the session each time and we listen to them discuss different areas which they think we might benefit from learning about. Tomorrow we are discussing blood pressure" Talia said, heels clicking again on the lino floor of the corridor.

"Is it always a GP that runs the session?" I asked.

"Yeah."

"Well, that doesn't seem right. What about Holly – she's a pharmacist and could probably teach the GPs a thing or two! Or even Rachel as a pharmacy technician? I mean – who created this elitist group that thinks only GPs can teach us something? Are we plebs?" I huffed, outraged at the idea that other professionals could be ignored in such a fashion. I imagined the indignation that Rosie would have when I phoned her that evening to tell her.

"Well, if you can teach us something then I'm all ears, you can do the next session then." There was a deep voice behind us in the corridor and we turned to stare. My heart sank as I realised that Dr Reeve had been eavesdropping behind us. *Did he ever actually do any work?*

"Erm, I'm not sure-" I stammered as he brushed past and held the door open for the both of us, still standing slack-jawed and staring at him. He smiled in a way that told me he was very much entertained by my discomfort.

"Oh but *I'm* sure. Welcome to the elitist club." Talia took the weight of the door from him, and he vanished as she turned to me with her lips smushed together, stifling a giggle.

"I walked right into that one, didn't I?"

Chapter FOUR

Josie

"So, you have to present in front of GPs, nurses, healthcare assistants, a pharmacist, a tech and god-knows who else?" There was a pause while I let her mull it over, knowing what was coming. "Oh sweet baby mother-"

"Yes. Me. ME." I sighed from the sofa at Rosie's house, having detoured there on my way home from work. She sat at the opposing end to me, feet propped on the sofa and ginormous bump very much present under a red knitted dress. One hand absentmindedly stroked her belly - the other covered her eyes as she groaned in horror.

"I mean, *I* wouldn't want to do that. God knows how you must feel." She opened her fingers and peeped at me; mouth set in a grimace.

"Look, I've been there two days and I already feel like some kind of imposter. I'm literally pretending to be knowledgeable. Eventually they're all gonna realise that I'm a big fraud and I know nothing. I mean what if I do this presentation and they laugh; what if they pity the pharmacy technician who pretended she knew something and knew nothing? I literally KNOW NOTHING!" I stopped to take a breath and looked at Rosie. She was sitting with worry etched into her face.

"Are you done or is there more to come?" She said and I shook my head. "Good. Ok. So, wow, where do I start with that?" She took a deep breath and began to stand up awkwardly and plod to the kitchen with one hand pushing into her back. I watched her grab two mugs from the cupboard, fill them with milk and plonk them in the microwave. Rosie's kitchen was what I'd describe as haphazard – it was clean but cluttered. The downstairs of the house was all open plan. Books and paperwork littered the dining table and there were boxes of what I presumed contained flat-pack baby furniture propped up against the far wall. She returned with two mugs and handed me a hot chocolate. "I've felt this too. I feel this every day I'm at work. I'll be standing and talking to a patient and thinking, *'what if everyone listening thinks I'm talking crap?'* and then I'll over analyse everything I said. I'll think that one day you're all going to realise I'm no good at this 'being a pharmacist' business."

"Really?" I said and she nodded. I sighed, "I don't even know where this has come from. One minute I'm me in the pharmacy and I feel like I'm there and I know what I know and the next I'm in this job where I know nothing but because of my job title I'm expected to know more. I almost don't want to admit that. It's hard to say it out loud and I just feel like *I* have become the elephant in the room. They all know I know nothing but none of them want to admit it and upset me."

"First of all – you know loads of stuff. You just need to learn the ropes in the job and get comfortable with processes. Second – this job is a learning job, so don't expect to know everything. Third – we always perceive things as much worse than they are. They do not think you know nothing; you just think they do."

"So what you're saying is-"

"They don't think that you know nothing. You just think that they think that you know nothing. They don't. And you don't." She sat back against the cushion and sipped the hot chocolate while I replayed her words in my head to make sense of what the hell she had just said to me.

"Erm...ok." I sipped on my hot chocolate too and there was a moment of silence before we looked at each other and started laughing.

"You have no idea what I just said do you?" She said, and I shook my head. "Basically, you're overthinking it all. You're fantastic and they will see that too."

"I hope so. Maybe it's just my period making me feel low." She passed me a teaspoon so I could scoop up the marshmallows.

"I am all over that, honey. Hormones had me weeping at a sausage roll yesterday – and it wasn't even that nice." We laughed and for a short time Rosie plied me with baked goods and more compliments. I really had no idea where this feeling had come from, but I needed to knock it on the head before it got out of hand.

"This Lexus dude…. I feel like I've seen the Reeve name on some prescriptions before. What's he actually like then?" She passed me the biscuit tin again. I explained as much as I could, trying desperately to paint an accurate picture of a man I barely knew but already had such a dislike for. He was arrogant, that was for sure. He probably knew he was attractive too which made me even more frustrated. He was probably one of those guys who thought he was above everyone else.

"You need to help me put my presentation together. I need to do a good job." I grabbed the sleeve of her dress in desperation.

"OK! Just maybe calm yourself, woman!" I let go and she raised her eyebrows at me. "He's really crawled under your skin, hasn't he?"

"Yeah. Ugh, I should probably go. Astrophe will wonder where I am. Give my love to Mike please." I stood and grabbed my coat, then leaned down to where Rosie sat and gave her an awkward half hug with added bump patting.

"Whatever you do Jos, don't accept being treated any less than you deserve."

*   *   *

"I'll refill the mugs so we can take a drink to training." Talia gathered them up and I stood to join her. I hadn't slept well, and the morning had been a tough one with at least two angry patients who I had been trying to help. My stomach felt a bit iffy and the thought of sitting in a room full of very clever people while simultaneously feeling like the obvious new girl, was making me feel a bit sickly. I so wished I could switch off the intense feeling of being terrible at this new job.

"Good morning, everyone, please sit." Dr Reeve greeted the group in front of me filing in through the door. As I passed him, he gave me a small, genuine smile. *How unnerving.* It took ten minutes for the room to fill and after many more introductions for me to various members of the team, the session began.

"Today I'd like to discuss with you all the management of blood pressure – it has been brought to my attention that we are not performing very well in this area as a practice. We are failing to monitor and act accordingly." I pulled open my notepad and poised my pen ready to make notes as he spoke. He didn't even seem like the same guy who had been taunting me for two days, he was smiling as he asked people questions and people genuinely seemed to like him.

"I love it when he wears that shirt." I heard a whisper behind me.

"Brenda, you're old enough to be his mother." Another voice hissed and there was a collective giggle.

"Did I miss something at the back? Josie?" Oh no. I felt all eyes in the room swivel in my direction and my heart began to race.

"Sorry Dr Reeve, I didn't hear."

"Is that because there was talking? Everybody - meet our new recruit – pharmacy technician Josie." He raised his eyebrows without hint of amusement and there was a smattering of greetings as I forced a smile and nodded. "Perhaps you'd like to introduce yourself?" *No, I really would not.* "Come to the front." I stood, feeling the heat in my face spreading down my neck, and my palms beginning to sweat. I couldn't even bring myself to look at the sea of faces and quickly focused on the back wall of the long room.

"Hi everyone, I'm J...Josie. I am a pharmacy technician from community pharmacy, and this is my first job in general practice." I rushed back to my seat and sat down. Talia smiled sympathetically at me, and Rachel nudged me with her knee.

"Welcome Josie. Josie has also very kindly offered to run the next training session." There was a silence that followed his revelation and then muttering broke out among the staff. A frowning Dr Cook leaned into Dr Ambrose and they both exchanged words and nodded to each other; two men who didn't seem to like what they were hearing.

"Ahem, Nick…can I ask what subject Josie intends to train us in?" Dr Cook asked – the news that a pharmacy technician was going to be running a training session seemed to displease a number of the crowd. *Think fast, think fast, think fast.* My mind raced for a topic. I would not be made to look stupid.

"Medication compliance aids and their place in the patient's care plan, Dr Cook." *Oh, hell was that me that spoke?* I looked at Dr Reeve whose brief look of surprise was quickly rearranged into a neutral expression.

"There we go. Right then on we go with the session." We sat for an hour and a half while various issues were raised. The nurses had a lot to say, and Holly raised some issues about medicines monitoring. I made so many notes that a dull throb started in my wrist. Dr Reeve didn't speak to me again and I could finally feel the flush in my face dissipating.

"Sorry you got singled out," Tina said as we reached the office afterwards. "Are you ok? You look like you've seen a ghost."

"I'm alright, just felt a bit nervous in front of that crowd." I said as I plonked myself down in my seat and pulled open my drawer to search for a snack.

"That was a great topic to choose, Josie!" Holly said as she burst into the office. "Nick seemed quite impressed. Let me know if you need any help."

The next couple of days passed quickly and though I was still learning how the practice functioned, I felt like my competency with the work was growing. I found speaking to patients was coming much more naturally and I was learning more about my colleagues. Rachel was keen on crochet, and I took great delight in examining the baby blanket she had crocheted for one of the reception ladies who was going on maternity leave. Tina was a whisky connoisseur and Talia thoroughly enjoyed having someone new to discuss the latest TV shows with. Holly's nails were painted intricately, and she shared some makeup vouchers with me, though I was sure I wouldn't be using them; makeup takes patience, and I could never be bothered.

By Friday, I was exhausted with the week's activities and more than ready for the weekend. Talia, Holly, Rachel, and I were sat logging onto our computers when Tina burst in and declared, "IT'S FIF ladies... IT'S FIF!"

"Hooray!" they chorused and I, momentarily stunned, was shown an open tin containing the biggest chocolate cake that I'd ever seen.

"Eff it Friday – every Friday." Tina said and I gasped as she winked mischievously.

"I brought non-alcoholic wine."

"I brought biscuits."

"I'm getting lunch – what'll it be? Chippy? Pizza?" They all turned to look in my direction and I was still taking in the food that was being placed onto the empty desk at the front. Rachel smiled, "Jos?"

"Oh, er, anything! Why do you have FIF?"

"Just our Friday treat – we're making this one extra special with it being your first week!" And make it special they did. By the time 5pm had rolled around, I was stuffed full, and the last member of staff in the office.

It seemed on Fridays I was going to be the one to finish latest of all the team.

I jumped at a sudden loud knock at the door as I was closing the blinds and turned to see the door swing open to reveal a familiar blonde-haired doctor.

"Oh, it's you." He said, not enthusiastically. "I was looking for Holly."

"Yes, it's me. She's gone." I said and returned to my desk to start packing my things ready to leave. He was standing, frowning and he leaned against the door.

"No-one else here?" He said and stepped inside, leaving the door to click closed in its frame. I made a show of looking around the room, as if to confirm it for myself before answering.

"Just me." He approached my desk, stopping by my side as I slid my diary into my bag. I could smell the aftershave again and almost didn't dare look up at him, for fear of blushing and embarrassing myself – it wouldn't do to give him the pleasure of seeing that I was clearly attracted to him. I could see the leather tops of his shoes in the corner of my eye and his hands appeared on the desk as he leaned down next to me and pushed his weight onto the table. Navy trousers and a crisp white shirt seemed to be an outfit that he favoured; I wasn't going to deny that it suited him.

"You will find that people do not appreciate you here." He said in a low voice, and I forgot myself and my eyes snapped to look at his.

"They won't?" I leaned across him to reach for my phone, not breaking his gaze and our arms brushed lightly.

"No."

"Why are you telling me this?" It seemed odd for one of the doctors to reveal that the practice lacked appreciation for its staff, especially to the new girl.

"You seem like the kind of person that will deserve appreciating. Just don't expect it." He said and I frowned as I swung my bag over my shoulder.

"I never expect appreciation and I don't do my job to be appreciated. I do it for the patients." I spoke haughtily; he had complimented me, but I didn't take it well.

"And therein lays your problem. You care too much." And then his face softened, and he smiled, a real genuine smile and I was momentarily thrown off guard.

"How is it possible to care too much, Dr Reeve? The patients should be our first concern, not politics or money." I leaned across him to log myself out of the computer and pull out my smartcard.

"Not everyone agrees with that and not everyone wants to see you succeed, Toyota." He looked at me honestly. "General practice isn't like community pharmacy."

I looked down at my feet, "And what would you know about community pharmacy? It isn't child's play."

"No. But you don't need to prove your worth in community pharmacy – here you do." He said and I shook my head in disagreement.

"Prove my worth to whom?"

"To the partners who said we didn't need another technician, who argued against using the funding for your job." He picked up my keys and passed them into my hand.

"Oh great – that's good to know." I said, my voice dripping with sarcasm. "Always good to start a job feeling welcomed."

"Oh, you are," he smirked, "I especially welcome new members of staff when they give me the middle finger on their first day."

"Well try and get up in my backside again and I'll give you more than the middle finger!" I snapped. There was a pause as he let me replay what I had just said inside my head and raised his eyebrows, a small smile playing about his lips. I felt my heart thud in my chest and said quickly, "I meant driving."

He stepped away from the desk, walked to the door and turned back to me with a grin. I was beet-red in the face as he stepped out of the door, and then peeped back round to ask, "Are you sure?" And then he was gone.

Chapter FIVE

Josie

I think the cat sensed my distress, or perhaps it was the absence of my snoring. It was 2am and I was still lying awake in the dark and unable to get Dr Nicholas-bloody-Reeve out of my damn mind. I wasn't a teenager anymore and I'd gone through more than my fair share of failed relationships, but why did this man excite me so? Astrophe head-butted my hand until I paid her some attention.

He was unpredictable and it was disturbing. He was a little intimidating, I admitted to myself, but it was kind of sexy. My last relationship had ended well over a year ago and I had ended it because he wasn't what I needed. I didn't know exactly what it was that I needed but I just knew it wasn't him. I used to be a happy singleton, much unlike Rosie before she and Mike had ended up together. I liked my own time and I liked being answerable only to myself. There was no need to make an effort for anyone and I could get away with eating a bowl of cereal for tea if I wanted to.

Having met a man who irritated and intrigued me, angered me and excited me, I suddenly couldn't help but feel like my home was too big for just me and the cat. It was too quiet. There suddenly felt like space had opened up in my life. I simultaneously wanted to avoid him and go and talk to him all in one tumultuous mix of feeling. The anxious feeling in my chest throbbed in response to my rising confusion.

I realised that I might *really* like him. How was it possible to be so attracted to someone after I only just met him? Ugh. He was kinda my boss too so that pretty much made him off limits – and who says he'd even like me? Oh god, what if he was already married or with someone? I sighed and thought that maybe the best idea would be to go about life as normal and pretend that I didn't fancy my new boss. Nothing could go wrong that way, could it? Astrophe meowed and jumped down from the bed, tail swinging haughtily. Perhaps she didn't agree.

*   *   *

I spent much of the weekend moping about, not really wanting to go anywhere. Even Rosie sensed something was up and I couldn't bring myself to tell her how stupid I was being purely based on a crush.

By the time Monday morning rolled around, I found myself feeling much less anxious as I sat in the office dipping a delicious cranberry and oat flavour cookie into a steaming cup of coffee, lovingly prepared by

Talia. Sunday night had been a revelation for me after watching a marathon of romance movies as the cold weather ramped up outside. It didn't seem to matter what happened in the movies, if the two characters were meant to be together then they ended up together. My life was not the movies, as much as I wished it was, and this was a silly crush because I was bored at home. I was going to have to consider socialising a bit more and take my mind off things. I was going to start tonight with a little home pamper session.

"Do you want to come with me on a home visit this morning?" Rachel asked me as she pulled off her coat by the door. "I'm doing a follow up on a patient that I visited with Holly last week."

How exciting! I immediately confirmed the obvious, that yes of course I'd love to go. There was something about going into a patient's house and seeing how we could help right there for them that made me giddy.

"Are you going to follow up on the blood pressure for Mrs Singh?" Holly asked her. I'd not yet gotten to know Holly as well as the others, she was often absent in this clinic or that meeting. She was lovely, just very busy. I'm sure she would help if I asked but so far, I'd had all my questions sorted by Rachel, Talia, and Tina.

"Indeed, we are – I'll ring if any concerns. We will leave around 10am in my car Josie." I finished my biscuit and got to work going through queries and calling patients. After only a week working at the practice, I felt like I'd learned so much already. From talking about how to take medicines, to liaising with community pharmacists and processing discharges from hospitals. It was so exciting being a cog in this huge wheel and still being able to see huge positive outcomes for people.

When 10am came along, Rachel ushered me out the door and to her car. She wore a woollen jumper over smart suit trousers and her shoulder-length brown hair shined in the winter sun.

"How do you get your hair so shiny?" I asked her and she laughed.

"Vinegar."

"What?!" I asked as I sat into the passenger seat.

"Just kidding. As a child my mum used to swear vinegar would make my hair shine and I had to wash my hair once a week in vinegar. Smelled foul. Nah – I don't really do anything now." She smiled and pulled out of the car park. I spotted the Lexus in its usual spot and quickly tried to think of something else to distract me.

"How bizarre. This lady we are going to see – what's going on there?" I asked.

"There's a laptop by your feet – you can fire it up while I'm driving if you want and take a look at her notes. You'll need to hotspot from your phone though." I pulled out the laptop and followed her instructions. "She was recently discharged after a heart attack – she has a lot of new medicines, and she wasn't taking much of anything before. Our plan is to check she knows what she's doing and recheck her blood pressure. Have you done training?"

I explained I'd done blood pressure checks in community and with the aid of the notes I now held on-screen as Rachel drove, we discussed the medicines and what had happened on the last visit she'd had with Holly.

We rounded a corner onto a winding country lane and the car rocked with the bumpiness of the road. Rachel turned the car into a driveway just over a rickety bridge, passing through an open red gate, and parked the car on a patch of gravel. The house was old fashioned with discoloured netting in the windows that made it seem dingy. It looked cold and uninviting.

"Hello? Mrs Singh?" Rachel called through the letterbox after there was no answer to the door knocking.

"Can I help?" A dark-haired man rounded the corner from the back of the house.

"Hi, I'm Josie and this is Rachel. We have an appointment with Mrs Singh; we are from the doctors' surgery?" We held up our ID cards to reassure him.

"She's this way – she's not so good really." We glanced at each other and followed him round the back of the house. He led us down a stone path lined with bushes and round to a conservatory door. When we got inside, Mrs Singh was sat bundled up in blankets watching TV. "She's a bit confused."

"Are you a relative of Mrs Singh's?" I asked him and he confirmed he was her son. We asked some questions and tried to talk to her, but she really didn't seem to be quite with it. Rachel was concerned because she was so different to their last appointment.

"Have there been any other symptoms?" Rachel asked.

"Not that I've noticed." He said. Rachel checked Mrs Singh's blood pressure while I went out to call Holly.

"She seems very confused – not at all with it. Her son states no other symptoms." I said into my phone.

"Well, I'll see what I can sort for an assessment for her today. Maybe the GP on house visits will check on her, I'll see who it is and have a word. I'll send you a text." Holly said and clicked off. I went back inside where Rachel was now going through medicines and looking at the boxes of what had and hadn't been taken. Her son was doing his best at explaining how he had been coming round to help her with them but in such a short time the packages were all muddled. Rachel started to take him through the medicines, encouraging Mrs Singh to talk where possible about them. My phone beeped.

Holly (10.35am):   GP on way, was seeing a patient nearby. X

Me (10.36am):   Thnx x

Just as Mrs Singh's son passed us a drink of juice, there was a knock at the door and I stood to answer it, shushing him as he tried to get up. Rounding the side of the house I caught sight of a familiar head of blonde hair.

"She's down here, Dr Reeve." I said and he turned in surprise to see me.

"You?"

"Yes, I'm on a house visit with Rachel. She's very confused, has been for a couple of days. It doesn't look like she's been very compliant with her meds. We didn't have a thermometer to check her temperature, but son says he hasn't noticed anything untoward. Rachel said she was completely lucid a week ago. We were here as she was recently discharged – I have the laptop open with the discharge inside." I chuntered as he followed me down the path.

"Right – thanks." He carried a brown leather bag and his grey overcoat swished along behind him. "Hello Mrs Singh, I'm Nick – one of the doctors. Is this your son?" He said loudly, a friendly smile on his face.

Rachel nudged me quietly as he spoke, "If Dr Reeve says its ok, we can go and arrange a follow up now we've sorted the medicines with her son."

"If you want to stay and Mrs Singh is happy with all these visitors, you don't need to leave on my account." Dr Reeve smiled at us as he pulled his thermometer from his bag.

"I really should go," Rachel smiled apologetically.

"And Rachel is my taxi, Mrs Singh, I'll be heading off too!" I started to put the medicines back into the box, but Dr Reeve interrupted.

"I'll give you a lift back Josie, then you can explain to me what is happening with these medicines." He said leaning towards her ear. I glanced at Rachel, eyes wide and she smiled and nodded in agreement.

"I'll see you in the office then." While Mrs Singh and Dr Reeve were distracted, I took her son once again through the medicines. He seemed to understand the timings and how better to support her and by the time it came to ensuring they were all put back into her box safely, Dr Reeve had decided on a course of antibiotics.

"Shall we?" He gestured to the Lexus in the driveway as we rounded the corner of the house.

"A Lexus... I'd never have guessed you drove one of those." I smiled in jest as I opened the back door to place my bag in. I was surprised to find two children's car seats and the confusion must have shown on my face as he threw his coat over one of the seats. At the other side. I placed my bag in the footwell of the nearest one.

"I have two daughters." He was unsmiling, guarding his expression carefully. Two daughters? How unexpected. A family man? I was thrown completely. He shut his door and waited for my response.

"Wow! How old are they?" Did this mean he was married? I reminded myself of last night's vow to keep it simple and revamp my own social life. It was none of my business. We climbed in the car, and it felt very tense. I played with my fingers in the absence of something to do.

"Six – they're twins." He started the engine and began to reverse the Lexus out of the driveway.

"That's…wow. A handful I can imagine. My friend is pregnant with her first, due any time in the next few weeks." I babbled.

"Mrs Singh will need a follow up. Can you make sure one is arranged when you get back?" He changed the subject, obviously keen for a new topic.

"Ah, yes of course." The rest of the journey back to the practice was near enough silent. I felt anxious to ask about the mother of his girls, but it felt too much like prying. The Lexus felt small and intimate, and the smell of his aftershave was once again overpowering. As we pulled into the carpark, he started to laugh.

"What's funny?" I asked.

"The Toyota. I laugh every time I see it."

"Don't let my Terry hear you laughing!" I snapped and he turned off the ignition and turned to stare at my frown.

"Really?" He raised his eyebrows and smiled. "Terry?" We both burst into laughter at how ridiculous it sounded, especially coming from him. "You make it sound like a 60-year-old man."

"You don't have a name for this lady then?" I said and stroked the side of my seat. He swallowed.

"No."

"Linda." I said and patted the dash.

"I am NOT calling my car, Linda." He unlocked his door as I laughed out loud from inside the car.

"Lorraine? Lola? Lavender? Lolita?" I called out the door as I undid my belt and climbed out. "I should start parking Terry next to her, give her some company."

"You think my car gets lonely?" He looked at me in disbelief as he pulled his coat from the car seat, and I leaned in to collect my bag.

"Well, I think she's a bit of a snob really. She needs someone like Terry to teach her how to lighten up a bit." I raised my eyebrows as I shut the door and he pressed the button to lock the car.

"I'm sure Terry could make all the difference to how she behaves then." He said as I followed him through the staff entrance.

"It will do her the world of good." I called behind me as I set off towards the office in the opposite direction to his room.

"Perhaps she could teach Terry one or two things herself." I heard him say as he turned out of sight. And despite my vow to stay out of his way, I smiled to myself knowing it was going to be quite impossible.

Chapter SIX

Josie

By Thursday, I was exhausted. For whatever reason, sleep had been evading me all week and I found myself feeling a bit antisocial and just trying to get through the working day without incident. I'd found the week challenging with queries I didn't feel confident with, patients being impatient and at times quite nasty, and having been ignored twice by the same GP, I felt a bit down.

Dr Cook was a man that seemed to be difficult to please. He had a smattering of brown-hair, a receding hair line and a constant look of disapproval – either that or a continuous foul odour under his nose. His response to my queries was almost always typed in capital letters, I never received a 'thankyou' or a note of guidance *and* I always got the sense he thought me stupid. The latest response I received to a query from him comprised of just three words: *'NO. ROUTINE APPOINTMENT.'*

It was disheartening to be learning a whole new job and doing my best, but also feeling like I didn't have the support of all my colleagues. I must have been staring into another dimension as it was Talia that interrupted my far away thoughts.

"Are you ok chick? You've been very quiet today." She said. Her hair was twisted into delicate curls and I could just see the hint of a tattoo on the inside of her wrist. She was incredibly pretty, good thing I wasn't the jealous type.

"You have, I was beginning to forget you were here!" Tina said. They both looked at me curiously and Rachel paused and turned to me too. Holly was absent in clinic.

"I'm fine! Just tired. It has been a pretty hectic two weeks and I've not been sleeping very well." I said and stretched in my seat.

"Coffee to wake you up?" Tina asked. I nodded but couldn't find my mug. Perhaps it was downstairs. I left the girls to pop down into the reception rooms to see if I'd left it when I went to scan on some documents. I was just making my way past the admin room when I spotted it in the kitchenette on the side. I rushed to pick it up, as if afraid it might run off.

"Tired, Toyota?" I should have known he wouldn't be far away. "Haven't seen you in a few days, have you been avoiding me?" Dr Reeve smiled as I turned to see him peering round the door from the corridor next to me.

"Just busy." I smiled half-heartedly, not really feeling up to our usual banter. I turned back to my mug and started running the sink taps. I heard the door close and suddenly he was next to me at the sink.

"Are you sure everything is alright? Not to be funny, Toyota, but you look like a bag of balls." He stated and I chuckled feebly as I looked at him. His face showed genuine concern, though. For whatever reason he wore scrubs today and I could see the edge of what looked like a tattoo under the neckline. He looked down at his chest, following my line of vision and back up into my eyes, smiling. I felt caught.

"I'm fine - busy couple of weeks and a lot to learn." I began rinsing my mug under the hot water, fully expecting him to leave but he was still standing next to me.

"Look, I know I'm not strictly 'on your team' as it were but I am the pharmacy lead. You can come and see me about anything." He said earnestly.

"Thank you. I'm totally fine." I said but we both knew it was without any conviction.

"So you say. Anyway, I hear Terry is getting on quite well with Lisa." He grinned and touched my shoulder lightly as he set off to the door.

"Lisa? Nice name, I hope she treats him right." I said, and there was a low laugh as the door shut behind him. After I finished washing my mug, I turned to walk back up the corridor and pass-through reception before heading up the stairs. But Dr Cook was there and suddenly my earlier musings about him thinking me stupid resurfaced, and I felt a little on edge. Should I approach him? He was standing, looking at a piece of paper near the filing cabinet, and frowning.

I suddenly felt a bit sweaty, what if he shouted at me? Or said something in front of everyone? What if he confirmed my fears that I really wasn't very good at this job? I shook my head and headed down the corridor anyway. He looked at me and looked back at his page, ignoring my forced smile by way of greeting.

"Afternoon Dr Cook." Silence. He continued to read his piece of paper, most likely pretending he hadn't heard me. *What on earth had I done to deserve being ignored?* I felt the knot of worry in my chest tighten. Maybe I didn't fit in here after all. The familiar cramping that signalled my period arriving was enough to make me feel a little tearful and although I managed to hold it together, by the time half past 5 rolled around, the girls were convinced there was something wrong.

"Are you sure everything is ok, Jos?" Tina asked me as we packed our bags ready to leave.

"Yes, Aunt Flo is visiting so I'm feeling a bit out of sorts." She nodded sympathetically and gave me a comforting hug.

I pulled Terry out of the car park and opted to call into the supermarket on the way home for some much-needed supplies. I was just debating between a chocolate eclair and a ring doughnut when there was a shrill call from my phone in my pocket.

"Where have you been, you've not answered my texts ALL DAY!" Rosie's familiar voice called down the handset.

"Oh Rosie, I was going to call when I got home. If I start talking now, I'm going to cry in the middle of the bakery aisle. Do I get eclairs or doughnuts?" I sighed.

"What's wrong? Doughnuts. But what's happened? If you're shopping for sweet supplies, then it constitutes an emergency."

"I don't think I can work there anymore. They hate me. They all hate me!" I whined. "There's a doctor who completely ignores me. I might leave. Will you have me back?"

"What?! No, I won't have you back because you need to go sort that doctor out and stand up for yourself!" I grabbed the doughnuts and the eclairs in desperation. "Tell me what happened!"

"I'm in the shop. I'm just going to go home and eat the sugar until I feel better. I'll call you tomorrow." I said to her.

"You know I love you Jos, right?"

I swallowed the huge lump forming in my throat. Hormones, over-tiredness, and work stress was making it very hard to speak without a sob. I whispered, "Yes." and clicked off the call. I took a deep breath and swallowed, now eyeing up the French Fancies as well but after a second to compose myself, turned to head to the checkout. And that's when I spotted him. Dr Reeve was standing behind me, loaf of bread in hand and near enough to have heard my entire conversation.

"Tell me what's going on." He said seriously and took three big strides towards me. I felt immediately stupid, like the drama I'd created was inconsequential and my hormones were criminals causing emotional chaos. I chuckled grimly and shook my head at his concern.

"I'm fine, just not feeling great. See you tomorrow, Dr Reeve." I said and set off down the aisle. I walked quickly to get away, scanned my items through the self-checkout and hurried out the shop door. I had just reached my car and plonked the food on the roof to search for my keys when his hand grasped my shoulder.

"Josie." I spun round in alarm to discover him out of breath and empty handed. He must have left his shopping. "Tell me. Has something awful happened?"

"No, Dr Reeve-"

"Nick."

"N-nick. I've just had a long week and not a lot of sleep." His hand was still on my shoulder and I was very aware that my back was against the drivers-side door to my car. It was cold and I was so very, very tired.

"You seem upset." He said.

"I'm fine." I insisted.

"What is it?" He demanded and he lifted his other arm to grasp both my shoulders tightly.

"Nothing!"

"I heard you say you're leaving." He said, looking straight into my eyes.

"I'm not."

"You can't." The sky was dark and there was a stillness in the carpark with the distant sound of traffic and his heavy breathing. Why was he so bothered that I'd leave? His hands were still gripping my shoulders tightly and I was suddenly very aware of how close our bodies were.

"Why can't I?" I dared to ask.

"Because-" He lifted a hand to run it through his hair, looked into the dark of the car park and shook his head. He seemed uncertain and I stood nervously, waiting. "We don't like to lose new staff." He let go of me, stepping back, and smiled sadly. "Enjoy your doughnuts." And then he was gone.

How baffling. I returned home with more on my mind than I set out with, scarfed down two doughnuts instead of an evening meal and put myself to bed on a concoction of painkillers. My troubled mind was out like a light, the day's exhaustion and events proving to be excellent hypnotics.

*   *   *

"You look a tad brighter today, Josie, if a little pale." Rachel commented as Talia pushed a fresh mug of hot coffee into my hands on Friday morning. I told them about my good sleep after a doughnut tea and Tina shook her head at me not looking after myself. Holly vowed to bring me in a portion of her special curry to try the following week and Talia opened her snack drawer and threw me a bar of low-calorie chocolate cereal.

I didn't mention how I'd been feeling about Dr Cook or what had happened with Dr Reeve. Although exactly what had happened last night, I wasn't completely sure. I checked which doctors were in work today and noticing Dr Cook was absent, my mood lifted considerably.

However, my lower belly ached and by late morning, I was also starving. Since the girls were busy on calls, I decided to send them all an instant message to ask what they fancied for lunch – I was going to treat them to FIF lunch this week. I quickly clicked down the list of names on screen so they all got the same message, and sent: *'Eff it Friday – my treat today. Taking votes on pizza or chippy. Ladies, you have a right to vote – use it! ;)'* I chuckled in spite of myself and pressed send. There were a couple of giggles in the room and Rachel whispered "Pizza!" and Tina gave her thumbs up to agree.

"What's this?" Talia asked, seeing us snickering.

"See your screen message...pizza or chippy for FIF!" I said smiling.

"Oh – you didn't send me one darls. But I'm good with pizza too."
I frowned in confusion, determined that I had sent the message to four people. If I hadn't sent it to Talia, who had I sent it to?

'Pizza sounds delicious – although I wouldn't call myself a lady. No pineapple, that's a sin.' Oh! It was Dr Reeve. I laughed out loud which drew curious looks from the girls; Talia leaned over to look at my screen.

"Did you offer Dr Reeve some FIF?!" She yelped.

"I must have sent it to him instead of you!" She burst into laughter and the other girls came to see.

"I guess my vote wouldn't have won – pizza it is!" Holly said, smiling. As they all settled into their seats, I considered whether I should reply. Did he actually want pizza? I presume he did, but should I respond? I ignored the message for a few minutes but Talia nudged me and insisted I reply.

'You can be one of the ladies today. Setting off at 12.' I replied and by the time I'd been out and returned with a selection of pizzas, I was positively ravenous. I carried the pizzas into the office and went to collect plates from the kitchen. Checking Dr Reeve wasn't seeing patients on the screen, I picked a couple of different flavours and carried a plate down to his room and knocked on the door.

"Come in!" he called, and I pushed it open and deposited the plate on his desk.

"Wow, thanks. What do I owe?" He looked for his bag.

"Nothing at all – I'm treating the ladies today." I turned to leave but he had stood and grabbed my hand before I could go out the door. I turned to look at him curiously, but he leaned past me and shut the door.

"Last night. You weren't good, what was wrong?" He said, pushing the plate away from the edge of his desk and perching on the end.

"Like I said, I was just tired Dr Reeve." He was still holding my hand. I was wearing one of my favourite outfits, a black pencil skirt buttoned up centrally to a high waist, with a lovely blue lace-patterned blouse neatly tucked in. The way he looked at me made me feel strange, my insides felt to be twisting with anticipation.

"Nick." He said heavily.

"Nick." I repeated. He looked at me, examining my face for answers and I observed his concerned expression, the stubble of his chin and redness of his lips. Suddenly, all I really wanted in that moment was to kiss him. His mouth was inviting, his eyes sparkled with excitement, and I have no idea what made me do it, but I stepped forward between his parted legs. He stared at my mouth and there was silence except that of our irregular breathing and the creak of the desk. I inched my face down to his, heart pounding and hands tingling. He was frozen still, his eyes followed my mouth as it neared him, and as I gently placed my lips against the fullness of his, both our eyes shut. For a second, I felt like I was falling.

I pulled away and opened my eyes, to discover him staring at me, unmoving and with an intense expression that I couldn't fathom. I must have made a mistake; I'd just kissed my boss! I stepped back in horror, but he stood suddenly and grabbed my shoulders, pushing me against the back of the door. I felt my head hit the wood and his body press into mine with fervour, pushing me roughly into the door. He laid his mouth on mine hard and suddenly we were kissing wildly, and I gripped his shirt almost as if I would fall if I let go. It had been so long since I had been kissed and I let out a breathy sigh as I felt his hands release my waist.

His fingers brushed up into my hair and I could feel the roughness of his chin as he moved his mouth against mine with a force that had me squeezing my thighs together. I pulled him by his shirt, wanting -no- *needing* him closer. I lifted my hands to touch his face and then almost as suddenly as the kiss began, I was released.

"No." He insisted as he stepped back and turned away from me. "I can't." *What? WHAT?* I sagged against the door, panting, and momentarily stunned. He wouldn't even turn and look at me. His head was bowed, and he didn't speak again as he moved to lean on the sill of the tinted windows. *He didn't want me?* He didn't want me.

A sudden flashback to that moment in high school when I'd been kissed for a dare by some stupid, childish teenage boy hit me, and the overwhelming need to leave had me yanking open the door and fleeing from the room without stopping to close it.

Going the long way round, I ran upstairs and straight into the bathroom to wash my face. I was horrified at what had just happened. Why had I kissed him? More to the point, why had he kissed me back and then rejected me? My heart sank when I remembered the car seats in his car, perhaps he was still in a relationship, and I had just kissed a married man? *Oh, the shame!* I splashed my face and wiped it, glancing in the mirror to compose myself. I *did* look pale. And now I had to go return to the office as if it had never happened at all.

I returned to the office and grabbed a lukewarm slice of pizza. The girls looked curiously at me but thankfully didn't comment. An instant message popped up on screen, *'Come back, please.'* I quickly deleted it, having no intention of returning to his room and humiliating myself further.

"How has today been then?" Talia asked me cheerfully, as she packed her bag to leave at the end of the day.

"I've learned a lot." *And learned a lesson.*

Chapter SEVEN

Josie

On Saturday morning, I encouraged Rosie to go for a walk to see if it would help bring labour on. She was 37 weeks pregnant, positively blooming, and very much sick of waiting. I came clean about what happened and my feelings about Nick Reeve. She was understandably as confused as I was about the whole situation.

"He must be married." She huffed as we paused for her to gather her breath, hands gripping her bump under denim dungarees. "Why else would he feel guilt at kissing you? Sounds hot though."

"It was." We started up our walk, waddle in Rosie's case, and amicably debated about the pros and cons of having a crush on a colleague. We reached the kids park and sat on the bench. "Look, that'll be you and Mike soon."

She looked in the direction I pointed; a couple cheered as their young daughter slid down a slide and we both sighed as she giggled with glee at the bottom. I pulled my hat further down my head and tightened my coat around me as the wind picked up. Rosie happily sat with her coat open, which was fortunate as it no longer closed over her roundness.

We watched as a group of children started climbing on the frame nearer to us, each trying to race to the top. A tall boy, maybe eleven or twelve, seemed to encourage them all to take bigger risks with climbing, and I watched with a mixture of fear and fascination. I was sure my daring had never extended to the heights that climbing frame did when I was so young. I was showing my age.

There was a sudden yell and I glanced up to the top of the frame to see a young girl dangling off with only her foot to stop her from falling. "Rosie, look!" She gasped as I stood in panic and ran to the frame while the girl yelled. I couldn't see her parents and panic set in – I had to help her.

"It's ok, I'm coming!" I grabbed the rope and pulled myself up without even thinking about the height.

"DADDY!" she yelled, and I could hear another girl calling to her from below. "HELP ME!" I hadn't the foggiest idea how I was going to help but all I knew was that she couldn't be allowed to fall.

"Hang on – I'm coming!" I climbed faster and further, my hands stinging and sore against the rope. Her hair swung and her face was pink with the cold, arms grasping at the air aimlessly. As I approached where she hung, her little upside-down face looked at me in fear. "It's ok. I'm

Josie, I've got you." I wrapped my arm under her shoulders and tensed myself as her weight pulled across onto me and she freed her foot, righting herself and grabbing for the rope as I held her.

"Ellie!" A male voice called from below and she gave me a faint smile as I put my arm around her and guided her down. As we neared the bottom ropes, she was lifted free from me, and I relaxed as I felt my feet hit firm ground.

"Thank you... you!?" I dusted myself off and looked up directly into the eyes of Nick Reeve himself with the girl in his arms, her features making her his double, with long beautiful curls framing her face, and clearly her twin sister clinging to his coat. He wore jeans and a jumper under the open coat and the unshaven face and glasses took me by surprise.

"Er, hi." I looked around, expecting to see their mother somewhere, but the other children had scattered and all I could see was the waddling figure of Rosie, a determined expression on her face as she approached us.

"Erm, girls this is Josie.... Josie this is Ellie and Eva." He nodded to each of the girls in turn and placed Ellie down next to her sister. They were so alike that I doubted I would be able to distinguish between them had they been dressed the same. Ellie tugged her dress down and leapt forward to wrap her arms around me.

"Thank you." Her voice said, muffled by my coat, and I knelt to her height.

"You're welcome – those ropes are scary, and you were super brave!" She smiled and I stood up as Rosie approached.

"Girls why don't you go play – not on the ropes." He said and as they ran off, smiled at me awkwardly. "Thanks for that."

I shrugged as Rosie approached, "Is everything ok?" She panted and grabbed the bench nearby to steady her.

"Yes, you shouldn't have rushed over!" She glanced at Nick and back at me with a curious expression. He smiled.

"Oh, er this is Dr Reeve, he's one of the doctors at work." I turned to him and gestured to Rosie, "This is Rosie, my best friend and former manager. She's a pharmacist."

Rosie's eyebrows rose so high they were in danger of disappearing, and I gave her a hard stare to warn her not to say anything at all. "Hi Rosie, what's it like working with Josie then? She's certainly made an impression on our team."

"Lexus." Rosie said and I paled, "You drive a Lexus." I gave her eye-daggers as he laughed and turned to me.

"Ah, so I'm famous?" He smirked and gave me a look.

"Yes, I hear you're a terrible driver." Rosie laughed and I held my breath, closed my eyes, and prayed she didn't say anything else. "Anyway, lovely to meet you but I've just seen the public toilets and my bladder won't hold any longer with the tap dancer inside here. See you in a minute, Jos." She nodded to Nick and set off towards the toilets just up the hill next to the playground.

"You didn't come back yesterday." He said after she left, and frowned. I cast around for something to say but couldn't find the right words to express my hurt at having been pushed away. "I'm sorry I pulled away, it's just-"

"Daddy!" His daughters came running across the playground and collided with his legs. He smiled apologetically.

"I know. You've got a family. I've already forgotten about it." I said and smiled at the girls. He opened his mouth to speak but I didn't want to hear it, "Lovely to meet you Ellie and Eva. Be careful on those ropes or your daddy will have to climb up for you next! See you soon." I left with a quick nod and headed in the same direction as Rosie. My chest ached at the thought that I was going to have to pretend it was alright, but I was crushed. There had been a fire between us, and I had stoked it thinking that something could happen.

"WELL!" She demanded as I caught her outside the toilets.

"Well, nothing. He has a family." I sighed, and she gathered me into a hug that only a best friend could give.

*   *   *

The following week at work passed quickly. Nick Reeve was thankfully out of office, presumably on annual leave, so I was free to think of anything but him. I wish I could say I didn't think of him once, but sadly I did keep wondering what he was doing with his time away. If the girls noticed my distraction in the office, they didn't comment.

I considered myself to be a bit of a sad sack when it came to dating history. There had been Rob as my first boyfriend – he was sexist, and I thought I couldn't do any better. Then, there was Ralph, and he thought he could make me into a fitness fanatic; when I finally decided to surprise him with an appearance at the gym, I discovered him lifting another woman onto his crotch rather than weights. Then, I had thought

Jon was the one. Jon was kind, he was caring and everything you could really ask for in a man. Sadly, it just got boring, and I felt like the only one with any spontaneity. I had started to think it was all over for me – I was going to be a cat lady and in a fit of madness had decided to adopt Astrophe as a kitten from the local shelter. Rosie had thought me hilarious.

She was positively livid when Friday came around and she hit her due date and had no baby to show for it; I listened to her on the phone for a full hour as she described exactly why being given a due date was predictably pointless. "And why can't men have babies because this is torturous! My breasts are like footballs, and I'm continuously convinced something is falling out of me!"

I was a very sympathetic and dutiful friend, but I couldn't help but chuckle to myself as she described her body. I lay under blankets by the TV, phone on speaker next to me and Astrophe commanding the space on my knee. The bloat this week was a result of a rather delicious cake we had all gorged on for FIF.

The weight gain concerns were real, and I had started to notice a correlation between my junk eating and anxiety. Dr Cook had been particularly nasty this week, refusing to help me with a patient I was really worried about, and it had left me more than a little confused and anxious. Holly had been off much of the week too, and we were snowed under with queries. Whenever I found myself needing a second opinion from a GP in Holly's absence, I started to feel a bit sick with nerves.

I don't know why it had become so bad, but the fear that they thought me stupid was too much, even thinking about it had me starting to shake behind my desk.

"Josie you've gone quiet, have I bored you to sleep?" I reassured her that I had not dozed off and I think she sensed I had lost the thread of the conversation. "What's up? Any news on Nick Reeve?"

"No – he's been absent all week." I said, "But I have my presentation next week so I really should be finishing it off. Can I send you the finished product to proof for me please?"

I balled my hands into fists to stop the shaking as I thought about standing up in front of the staff and seeing Dr Cook there, knowing full well he had no interest in what I had to say. I wasn't sure I dared do it, but if I backed out now then I was sure to look a coward.

"You know I will, only labour will stop me." We finished talking, and when I clicked off the call, Astrophe had started massaging my bloated belly, tugging on the blanket with her mouth as she did it.

"Oh, baby girl – your life is so simple." I said to her, unmuted the TV and shakily reached for the glass of gin that waited for me on the side.

Chapter EIGHT

Josie

On Tuesday night, the eve of my presentation, I decided that a confidence boost was in order. I was going to prepare myself the only way I knew how: bath soak, hair wash, hair removal and glass of something cold – maybe not in that order.

Ice cold glass of cheap wine from the local newsagents on the bathroom sink, hair removal cream sprayed on my spread legs, sitting naked on the toilet lid with a pack of hair dye soaking in under a shower cap, and reading the latest shitty gossip magazine was the height of pre-presentation preparation.

I was just reading about Angela in Astbury and her extra-marital affair with her neighbour's brother, when a sensation on my leg startled me and I discovered Astrophe rubbing her side into my legs. I chuckled and scratched the tip of her head before she trotted off with big patch of white cream on her side. She was going to need a wipe to get that cream off once I'd done.

I returned to the magazine and the discovery of Angela's adultery, when the image of Astrophe trotting out of the bathroom with cream on her side swam across my vision and my heart skipped a beat.

"ASTROPHE!" I yelled. It was hair removal cream – I was going to have a bald cat! I dropped the magazine and set off looking for her out of the bathroom. Catching sight of a tail whipping round the doorway into the bedroom, I followed as quickly as I could without touching anything. "Come on big girl, come on!" I urged her. I was naked, my only covering consisting of a shower cap, the stains of hair dye behind my ears and cream covered legs below the knee. Thank God I lived alone.

My room was a state. Clothes chucked on chairs, hung on curtain poles, a pile on the floor and I dodged the bed, not wanting to spread the cream further, and spotted her tail slinking underneath. I couldn't kneel, the cream would get everywhere! I had to get her out somehow and resigned myself to washing my legs before the ten minutes was up, and dragged her out to clean her.

"Is hair removal cream toxic to cats?" I asked Rosie on the phone while I soaked in the bath later, my hair a little darker than I had intended given I'd left the colour on too long while trying to coax the cat out. I'd discovered her licking at the fur, not sure if she had actually tasted any cream and I had maybe been a tad forceful with washing her.

"I blanked my veterinary pharmacology lectures – but I'm fairly sure it's toxic to anyone who chooses to eat it." She said. I doubted that

Astrophe would come near me for a long time, she had hidden under the sofa and I was happy to leave her there, the scratches on my arms testament to our disagreement. "How are you feeling about the presentation tomorrow?"

Scared. No – terrified. Dr Cook's face swam in front of my eyes, his receding hairline and disapproving frown present for effect. It would be a room full of all the clinical staff, including the pharmacy team I had only recently become part of. It was absurd that I should be the first non-GP to present, and I wanted to do it well enough so that others could do it too, after me.

"Ask me tomorrow when it's over." I said dryly.

"You'll be fine. What are you going to wear?" She said, sounding tired. I had debated with a trouser suit but it felt like I was trying too hard. I considered a skirt, but my favourite skirt now reminded me of the kiss I'd shared with Nick Reeve who, by the way, I hadn't seen since the park. I wasn't entirely sure if I wanted him at the presentation. Either he would be a distraction or a voice of reason – who knew anything when it came to that man? I shuddered as I remembered the roughness of his face against my cheeks and the push of his hands into my hips. He was so deliciously unavailable, and my chest ached.

"The black swishy dress – I'll pair it with a blue cardigan." I decided.

"Good choice," Rosie yawned and I insisted she go to bed – she was going to need as much sleep as possible before baby arrived. The phone clicked off and I climbed out of the bath and dried myself before heading to my bedroom and trying not to think of tomorrow.

"Astrophe?" I called as I switched the light off and slid into the covers. Her usual mew followed by the nightly purr never came and I laid in silence and awaited the morning.

*   *   *

"Wow, what happened to you?!" Tina said as I burst through the door on Wednesday morning. She handed me a steaming coffee that was clearly freshly made anticipating my arrival. "You look shattered...gorgeous but shattered!"

I gratefully accepted the coffee cup and Rachel passed me a croissant from a pack on the side. "She was up all night worrying about this presentation, you can see it in the circles under her eyes."

"Yes – I'd be lying if I said I wasn't anxious." I was at the point of fight or flight, prepared to leave at any moment. I stared into the murky coffee and imagined how it would feel just to dive in and forget that work existed. I tried imagining myself eating the very same croissant on a hotel balcony, sparkly sea as the backdrop to a perfectly presented breakfast in deliciously skin-warming sunshine.

"I'd suggest we swap FIF to today, but I think we will need it on Friday." Tina said and I booted up my computer. We had the morning to work before the presentation and concentration was out of the window.

"How are you feeling about presenting, Josie?" Holly asked. She looked gorgeous today, sleek, and shiny hair and a dress that cut in all the right places. My colleagues were very beautiful people. I looked down at the black dress I had worn for the occasion and suddenly felt tatty by comparison. I smiled weakly in response.

"Right then missus, it's time." Rachel nudged me a couple of hours later and I sucked in a shaky breath when I noticed the clock. I was more than likely blowing this all out of proportion, but teetering down the steps towards the meeting room felt like I was on course for disaster.

"Wow, you look amazing!" came a voice from beside me; Janice was one of our nurse practitioners sliding out of her consultation room.

"She does, doesn't she?" Talia's voice came from behind. The click of my heels and swish of my dress was more purposeful than I intended and the nearer we got to the room, the faster my heart began to beat.

"Ooh, it looks very busy!" Rachel said from up ahead. "We might be standing, ladies." I felt so sick. I was sure to say something, anything that made no sense or was wrong. I had no place here. I stopped abruptly and Talia almost walked into me.

"I can't." I hissed at her.

"You can. You know what you're talking about, and we are right here. If they ask something and you don't know the answer and one of us does, we will pipe up! Go on. Walk in there with your chest out and your pert little butt following." She nudged me forward and I swallowed as I walked in and the eyes in the room collectively turned to look at me.

There was one pair of piercing blue irises that I got caught up in very quickly, and the intensity of his stare and the way he took his time examining me in this dress was enough to bolster me to keep going. I could not look a fool in front of him, but after looking away, I knew I couldn't look at him again or I might lose my nerve.

My presentation was already preloaded onto the screen – courtesy of Anne – and I took my place in front of the crowd, and was momentarily thrown back in time to being the little girl at school who had been told to be quiet on stage. *Deep breath.*

"Good morning, everyone. Just to reintroduce myself: my name is Josie and I am the new pharmacy technician here at the practice. My background is primarily community pharmacy and my experiences of inappropriate use of multicompartment compliance aids are one of the reasons I wanted to discuss this with you today." A pin could have dropped, and we would all have heard it.

I began telling my audience about how requesting medicines for community pharmacies to put into trays for patients wasn't always the best option and felt my confidence grow as I shared examples of when this had led to errors or patient dosing mishaps. I described the effort required to dispense medicines in this way by community pharmacies and the lack of remuneration for the service.

"If we want our services in prescribing medicines to be done appropriately, we should be working closer with our community pharmacy colleagues in assessing patient suitability. They see our patients more often than we do and we can learn a lot by working with them." I rounded off my presentation. There was a round of applause, perhaps a little overenthusiastically by my team in the back row and Dr Cook leaned forward as the sound faded away.

"That's all very well and good Miss, but there is nothing in our contract that states we need to work with community pharmacists – so why waste our time." He reached for his jacket.

"Well actually-" I paused, suddenly realising I was about to contradict one of the most intimidating men that I had ever met. I glanced at the girls and they nodded to encourage me to go on. "The formation of primary care networks was to encourage better integration and service provision. The service specification states that we must work with our colleagues in community pharmacy. And even without that requirement, patient safety is at risk here and it is our duty to put our patients first."

"Well, Miss. Is that over for today? We have more important work to do." And to my disgust he stood and left, followed by a number of fellow GPs, a couple of nurses and some of the admin staff. I felt deflated.

"Thanks all for attending and if you have any questions, please feel free to come and ask." I turned to the computer to turn it off, but it was opportunity to hide the disappointment in my face.

"I don't think we've met?" A rather tall and dark-haired chap approached me, the glasses perched on the end of his nose giving him a look of a slightly rougher Clark Kent. "I'm James, a locum GP".

"Oh, hi James! Nice to meet you." He shook my hand firmly and I took in the un-ironed scrubs and five-o-clock shadow across his cheek. He followed my gaze and grinned.

"I came straight from nights at St James's, I'm going home now. I just wanted to say that I really enjoyed your presentation. I think it's great that Nick is inviting others to present, especially when skills like yours are invaluable." He seemed genuinely pleased to have listened to my presentation! *Result!*

"I'm working Tuesday and Thursday next week, you'll have to pop down and say 'hello'." But before I had chance to talk any more, I was ambushed by Talia, Rachel, and Tina; James smiled and disappeared behind them.

"That was amazing!" They gushed over the presentation and although I argued Dr Cook had ruined it, I was secretly pleased that James had complimented it. If I impressed one GP, then surely some of the others would have felt it was useful too. Nick's seat was empty and when I glanced at the door, I caught him leaving with a thunderous expression on his face and sighed.

"What's up chick?" Tina asked.

"Dr Reeve said nothing at all and just left. He looked pissed." I said as we made our way back to the office.

"Take no notice. You smashed it in there, he probably wanted you to fail." I doubted that. I doubted it very much. I wanted to impress him, but apparently all I'd done was make him angry. I returned to the office feeling like a failure and grumped my way through the next lot of tasks.

Later, there was a knock at the door, and I jumped out of a reverie and splashed coffee on my arm, mid-drink. The door opened slowly, and Nick Reeve peeped his head around. "Afternoon, all." He nodded as they greeted him but then caught my eye as I wiped my hand with the tissues from my desk. "I need a word."

I nodded and followed him, with a quick glance to the girls. Talia was positively bursting with curiosity; I could see her nudging Tina and knew that as soon as the door closed behind me that they'd be muttering. He had set off down the corridor and was pushing on door handles and shaking his head upon discovering they were locked. His trousers were tailored just a little more tightly than was strictly necessary, although I might consider them a little tighter than was strictly professional, and the blue shirt, which had become my favourite, complimented the blonde hair I still wanted to run my fingers through.

At last, he reached a doorhandle that clicked open and disappeared inside without a backwards glance. My heels clicked along the corridor and the black work dress worn especially for the presentation swished around my knees, but neither of these gave me confidence for whatever I was about to hear him say, he had been frowning when he asked for a word, hadn't he? I glanced up and down the corridor before pushing the door open.

"Shut the door." He said sharply. It was no bigger than a storeroom, shelves either side lined the walls and a sink sat against the window which, given the orientation of the building, I presumed overlooked the car park. I clicked the door shut and turned to where he stood, hands either side of the sink and staring out of the window.

"Dr Reeve-" I began.

"*Nick.*" Silence. He gripped the sink very tightly and I struggled to find words to speak. Had something about my presentation angered him? I sucked in a breath to speak but, "I'm so angry."

"I'm sorry." I said and took two steps forward.

"You should be. Two things. You should not have been spoken to like that by Dr Cook." It came out like a growl, and I was surprised. Had my presentation caused this many issues? Legs trembling, I wrapped my arms across my front as if to hold myself together. "He was out of line. But the second thing is one hundred percent your fault."

"What can I do to make it better?" It barely came out as a whisper.

"Never wear that dress to work again." *Pardon? Did he just say dress?*

"Wh..what?" He turned slowly, letting his grip of the sink go and closed the remaining gap between us. His hands grasped my waist and with a possessive look in his eyes, shook me lightly.

"Don't. Wear. This. Dress." He snarled, his grip tight around my waist and I was trembling with confusion. Everybody had seemed to like the dress, or at least the girls had paid me some lovely compliments. Even Damien the trainee had said I looked smart!

"I don't understand. But the dress-code-"

"FUCK the dress-code!" He snapped. His eyes were wild, nostrils flaring and the shirt he wore was pulled incredibly tightly across his chest muscles which were fighting to break free. This was a new side to Nick Reeve that I had never seen before.

"Dr-" I began

"Nick. Why can't you call me by my name?" He let go of my waist and ran his fingers through the hair I'd happily fantasised about only moments earlier.

"You're my boss, I'm trying to be respectful. I'm sorry you don't like my dress, but I must go." I turned to leave but before I could open the door, he had his hand on it holding it shut.

"It isn't that I don't like the dress." He said quietly. "Do you like me?"

Facing the door, with him behind me holding it sealed shut, it felt like a trick question. I knew my answer, of course. But what if it wasn't the answer he wanted to hear?

"What?" I said, my body still, eyes firmly on the white paint that was chipped on the doorframe.

"Do. You. Like. Me?" He repeated, though it was clear his patience was wearing thin, like an over tuned violin string, ready to spring free and snap.

"Yes." And I did. He took a step closer, cocooning us in the smell of his aftershave, and pulled his hand from the door to pull strands of my hair off my shoulder and expose my neck.

"Do you…want me?" I gasped as his mouth touched my neck and his arms pulled me back into his solid body. I closed my eyes as his teeth nipped at my ear and his hands pulled at the skirt of my dress. I exhaled roughly as he ran a hand up the inside of my thigh and a finger caught in the lace of my underwear. "That's not an answer."

He grabbed one of my hands and placed my palm against the door, mirroring it with the other and leaning round to twist the lock under the handle. Nudging my feet open with his foot, I felt him kneel behind me, hands exploring the insides of my legs and teasing as I bit my lip. With each stroke he climbed higher up inside of my thighs. *We could get caught.*

"I asked a question." He lifted my dress to expose my rear and bit my cheek; I gasped.

"Yes!" And as soon as the word was out, he stood, pulled me to face him and pressed his mouth onto mine in a brief, rough kiss.

"We should go." And in that second, he was a different man entirely. He leaned round me to unlock the door and I stepped to the side in bewilderment as he opened it to let me out again.

"Wait-" I said, not really understanding anything at all.

"The presentation was great." He said formally as he stepped out of the storeroom, "Thanks for showing me where the prescriptions are stored now." Amanda from admin was approaching from down the corridor. We shared a look after she passed us.

"But the dress?" I whispered as he started to walk away.

"I love it. I just don't love watching other people see you in it."

Chapter NINE

Josie

"What happened?" Rosie said and I pictured her on the edge of her seat.

"We err. We…." I gripped the phone as I patted Astrophe's head on the sofa. It would seem I was forgiven for the shaving cream incident.

"Did you?" There was a gasp. "You didn't!"

"No! We didn't. Not that." I insisted, somehow understanding the incoherent babble between us.

"But did he? And did you?" I pulled at the tatty edge of the sofa while I contemplated what she asked, for even this was testing my ability to converse in nonsense.

"If you're asking what I'm thinking then no and no." I laughed as she sighed with disappointment. Anything for a bit of gossip and we were two harpies in a den, happily picking at people like scraps of meat. To find myself the subject of said gossip was novel and yet I couldn't help but feel a simmering of giddy excitement about this secret office flirtation. From Mr Lexus to Dr Flirt – the changes in his personality had ignited a rush of *something-something* and I curled my toes under the blanket as I thought back to the tightness of his muscles as he had tried to control himself in the cupboard. *He was holding back on me.*

"Earth to Josie!" Rosie's shrill voice rang through the phone speaker, and I jumped, Astrophe making a quick getaway.

"Yes, sorry." I finished my call with her and reached for my drink, a large glass of lemonade that was neither cold nor refreshing.

It occurred to me that Nick Reeve could be playing a game with me and for a moment I contemplated his motives. But then the image of those two girls in the park refocused my thoughts and I gripped the glass tightly – I still didn't know if he was married! I'd check social media – surely there would be traces of him. I put down my glass and grabbed my phone, fumbling over spelling as I typed in 'Nick Reeve' into the people search box. Nothing. 'Nicholas Reeve'. Ten of them appeared, but the first picture was his recognisable blonde hair and a blissful smile on his gorgeous, tanned face while he stood topless on some beach or other. I sighed as I zoomed in to the picture, enjoying my snoop but eager for more titbits of information about him. There was a cover photo with his girls, clearly an old one for they were only babies, and *darn it,* the profile information was hidden. I scrolled to see what I could find, inside secretly knowing that if I found something it would serve as punishment for snooping.

Aha! And there it was – a wedding picture – and, oh, she was beautiful. Decorated in a beautiful white lace, princess-style wedding dress, stood a stunning woman gripping his hands as he gazed adoringly at her. His beautiful, chiselled, awed face looked at her with an expression I had only ever dreamed of experiencing. His wife. His *wife.* HIS WIFE! My gut clenched and a feeling of nausea overcame me. I closed my phone screen in disgust and threw it at the cushion on the opposite end of the sofa where it landed with a muted thud and tumbled off the side.

I was defeated. The tiny wisps of hope that had once signalled newfound kindling of romance were gone and I felt crushed that I had let myself be humiliated by a married man. How *dare* he? Had he no shame? He had clearly not thought that I would discover his relationship, I mean it hadn't taken a private detective, had it? I felt cheap and used, retrieved my phone to text Rosie the bad news, and stomped off for a shower.

"What a sanctimonious bastard." I spat under the shower, not really knowing what the word meant but it sounded insulting, and he deserved it. He deserved everything and nothing all at once. By the time the water had turned cold, and my fingers resembled those of one of my earlier patients, I was truly all angered out. I would not – could not –

create a fuss. I would dismiss his advances, if he continued to offer them

of course, and continue with my career.

My career was already a fight to establish myself and messing

around with one of the partners was not a good way to start. No, no.

Fresh eyes from tomorrow. And having scrubbed my body within an inch

of its life, I slipped my pink-tinged legs into my pyjama bottoms, pulled on

a baggy t-shirt and sank into bed. Sleep overcame me almost

instantaneously, mind exhausted with the day's events.

*   *   *

"Would you take a look at this discharge, please Josie?" Talia said.

A box popped up on the screen and I opened the patient's record to begin

examining the discharge letter from the hospital. The patient had been

admitted after a fall and some of the blood pressure medicines had been

stopped. It looked like the patient's low blood pressure had contributed –

they had been overmedicated.

I began picking apart what needed changing, happily documenting

in the patient's record the details of the admission and planned medicines changes. It was a big discharge, by all accounts, and it took a lot of concentration such that I lost awareness of my phone ringing.

"Hello, Josie's phone." I turned in shock to see Rachel holding my phone, "Oh, hi Dr Reeve." I shook my head furiously at her and mouthed, 'Nope – toilet!' while pointing at the door. "Sorry, she's gone to the bathroom. Yes, I'll tell her you want a word."

"Thanks, Rach." I sighed and turned back to the computer.

"I thought you needed the bathroom?" She frowned at me, concerned.

"Can we talk later?" I whispered and nodded to the others who were taking calls around us. She agreed. I needed time to work out what I was going to say. A box appeared in the corner of my screen, *'Dr Nicholas Reeve 10:09: Please can you come down to my room.'* I clicked the 'dismiss' button and carried on.

I removed a medicine from the list of medicines on repeat and documented why it was being removed, *'Dr Nicholas Reeve 10:14: Are you being deliberately elusive, Toyota?'* I clicked 'dismiss' again, teeth grinding in frustration, and stood to pay a visit to the bathroom.

"So…you are avoiding me?" His voice echoed down the corridor as I passed the door behind which he had seduced me only the day before.

"I'm busy." I continued to walk towards the upstairs bathroom, not even turning to look at him.

"You weren't busy yesterday." His voice was deliciously silky and seductive, but I could not let myself cave. I continued to walk, and his footsteps grew more purposeful, louder, and nearer. As my hand brushed against the bathroom door, he threw his arm across the doorway and slipped between me and the door, knocking my arm aside.

"Don't walk away from me." He commanded and I stepped back with the force of his voice.

"Then don't be such a lying pig." I looked him in the eye as I spoke and his eyes widened in shock, his mouth falling open. "I don't think your wife would want you messing with one of your staff, do you?"

There was a beat of silence as his expression transitioned from shock to something which looked like anguish before hardening to a look of restrained fury. He turned sharply and slammed his hand into the bathroom door, swinging it open, before striding away without a word. I exhaled as he rounded the corner and the door swung shut in its frame and made me jump.

Rachel was clearly curious; she asked me what was going on when I returned to the pharmacy office. My explanation that I had forgotten to research a patient for his query didn't seem to fully satisfy her as to my dismissing his call, but she kept her thoughts to herself.

I turned to my computer and began work again, working through a list of clinic letters with medicines recommendations from specialists. Suddenly, my phone began to shrill loudly which distracted me from any thoughts of wayward doctors and intimate regrets, an incoming video call from Rosie. *She knows I'm at work...* I shuffled into the corridor as I swiped up the screen, and promptly gasped as I was greeted by the face of a freshly birthed, beautifully puckering up baby, complete with thatch of dark hair and miniature wrinkled fingers clawing a hospital towel.

"OH MY GOODNESS!" I yelled and pressed my hand to my open mouth. "Hello, little one!"

"This is Annie Mae." The pride in Mike's voice as he introduced their daughter made my heart ache, and the camera moved out to focus on Rosie's pale but serene face.

"She is beautiful! Oh, my goodness, I can't quite believe it! Congratulations, both of you. Well done, Mama!" I stared at the squidgy baby girl as Mike gushed about her, while Rosie remained uncharacteristically quiet as she took in the baby in her arms. What a precious moment!

"How are you doing?" I said to Rosie.

"I'm tired, but she's worth it." She sighed. "Will you come visit when we get home?"

I assured the smitten parents that I would indeed visit as soon as they felt up to visitors, and that I would bring any shopping they needed with me.

I slid back into the office, with a delighted grin on my face, and announced to the office that I was an honorary aunt to a beautiful baby girl.

"That's amazing!" Tina clapped.

"What's amazing?" Talia caught the tail end of the conversation as she made her way in with a round of freshly-filled mugs. I shared the news again and –"That IS good news, congratulations! I tell you who could do with some good news – Dr Reeve – he's in a right foul mood today. He just shouted at me because I spilled the tea on the side – I did wipe it!"

The smile dripped off my face and I glanced at Rachel, almost reflexively, and she raised her eyebrows at me as Talia distributed the mugs.

"He's a bar steward that one. A right bar-steward." Tina said in a broad Yorkshire accent.

"A fit one though..." Talia stated simply, and they all giggled.

A box popped up on my computer screen alerting me to the delivery of a new task to my inbox. It was from Dr Cook, presumably a response to the query I sent him about a patient allergy and a discharge request to prescribe the same drug; my heart began to tap dance with nerves as I clicked open his response.

*'It would seem that you are incapable of dealing with this yourself. Perhaps instead of wasting MY time, you ought to consult with a pharmacy colleague who actually **knows what they are doing.'***

I read it three times before it sank in. He thought me incapable because I asked him a question? He thought me incapable because I expressed my concerns about a request to issue a patient with a medicine that they were documented as allergic to? My understanding about this role was that I would be supported, not ridiculed. I had discussed my ideas with Holly and presented my thoughts about the case to him, and here it was in black and white: apparently, I didn't know what I was doing.

"Are you ok Josie?" Holly asked me.

"Erm, I'm not sure. Do you remember Mrs Wadley? The lady with the clinic letter from urology requesting long term trimethoprim?" I said.

"Ah yes, the lady with the allergy?"

"Yes. I received a response, but Dr Cook said to ask a pharmacy colleague as he didn't have the time." I paraphrased to leave out the unpleasant parts of his message. There was a collective groan among the team and Holly frowned in disproval, and offered to take over the patient's management for me.

"I'll let you know the outcome, lovely, don't worry. Sometimes the doctors just like efficiency and Dr Cook can be quite impatient, that's just his nature."

I nodded but far from agreed with the sentiment. So...I should just accept being spoken to like that? My heart gently sank in my chest, along with my mood and any self-confidence I had. Another 'ping!' and I was alerted to yet another task response from Dr Cook in my inbox.

'YES. Why are you wasting my time asking?'

I took a moment to compose myself, took a deep breath, and pulled open the patient record to deal with the plan I had originally outlined, and that Dr Cook had so rudely agreed to. He clearly thought me stupid, and I was starting to feel nervous to ask him questions for fear of being excoriated.

When the end of the day creeped up slowly, I sighed as the others left one-by-one until only Rachel and I remained packing up together.

"Is everything ok, Josie?" She enquired as she logged her computer off.

"It hasn't been a very good day today, Rach. I don't feel like I've done a very good job." She approached my desk, looking incredibly smart in a green wrap dress and black heels, and exhaled as she sank onto the edge of the table.

"Some of our colleagues aren't very supportive… you may find. And sometimes it can get tricky when you find yourself without an answer and needing to ask another colleague because the first refuses to help." She said gently and slowly, weighing up each word with undertones of caution that suggested she spoke from experience.

"I thought I'd be happy here…" I whispered, feeling my eyes fill with tears.

"You can be happy with us; we will always support you in our little team in here." She stood and draped her arm around my shoulder. "We might not always have full support, but we will do what we can between us all and we will still keep smiling. Come on, let's get out of here."

We grabbed our bags, and I flicked the lights off as we left. I was still holding back my tears and as I reached my car, Rachel enveloped me in a tight hug and dabbed my eyes with a tissue from her pocket, promising it was clean and that things would be ok.

"Chin up, lovely. Things could be worse." She smiled gently and tapped me on the chin. "I'll see you next week."

I watched her return to her car and gently slid into my own driving seat, only to hear the engine of the car next to me spring to life. Knowing full well it was *his* car, I stole a glance across the windows and our eyes caught. The frown on his face softened, if only for a second, and in a moment of weakness my resolve to remain distant faltered and I grabbed the door handle as if to climb back out of the car. But alas, before I could even pull on the handle, his features returned to angry again and his engine roared as he pulled the car out of the car park and I was left staring at his car parking space, the sign declaring 'Doctor' doing anything but make me feel safe or cared about.

Suddenly the confines of community pharmacy, of baskets and controlled drugs balances, date checking and dispensing, and the familiar work family that I had grown to love, felt so far away. My heart ached as I drove home, not really knowing who to call or what exactly I could say.

Chapter TEN

Josie

"Josie, you're due a review." Holly said as I hung up the phone one Monday morning. "Nick needs to do your probation forms."

Two long weeks had passed since I had confronted Nick about his wife. And for two weeks neither of us had spoken, only perhaps through tasks relating to patients, and it was all very formal. Nobody in the office had had reason to suspect anything, and I had very much kept my thoughts to myself about everything that had gone on between us.

In truth, I wasn't holding up very well, which was most unlike me. I had always considered myself to not be a 'stressy' person, taking things in my stride and always just plodding along regardless of the behaviour of others. Now, I was more than just 'out-of-sorts', I was a bit of a mess.

My communications with Dr Cook had become fewer, though nastier, and I had taken to dreading ever needing to ask for his support. I lived for the end of the day and had developed a habit of driving home the long way, to avoid having to sit at home alone and wallow in my own sadness and insecurities. I was 34, a grown woman, and yet feeling like much more akin to a lost kid in need of a hug.

The years of dedication I had given to my job had earned me solitude and stability, something I had always been content with. But now that my only close friend was busy with her own family, and I was suddenly realising that pretending I wasn't attracted to Nick Reeve felt virtually impossible, loneliness had set in.

"Josie?" Holly's voice penetrated the haze of meandering thoughts, and I shook my head as if to shake them away.

"Sorry Holly, what time does he want me and where?" She gave me his number and asked me to text him, since apparently, he was busy all afternoon and had to find a time that was convenient.

Having a review session with him when we hadn't spoken in so long, and when our last conversation still felt so raw, wasn't something I was going to look forward to.

Me (11:47): Holly informed me that I'm due a review with you this afternoon. When would you like to meet? Josie.

Nick Reeve (12.17): I am on home visits this afternoon, but I will message when it is convenient, and I am on my way back.

"What happens in a review?" I whispered to Talia, whose hair was uncharacteristically plain blonde. "And where did last week's purple go?"

"They just usually ask how you're getting on, provide you with feedback and document it all. Unless you've been naughty, you've got nothing to worry about!" She winked.

"And the hair?" I pushed.

"Sadly, Anne thought it inappropriate for work and distracting for patients, not that I see any patients face to face mind you!" She shook her head sadly.

"You don't look like you without the vibrant colour." I reached out and pulled on a strand of her hair.

"It'll be back for one night and one night only! You haven't forgotten our night out, have you?" She squirmed with excitement in her seat.

"I bloody hope she hasn't, it was organised in her honour!" Tina said loudly and smiled. "I'm going with a new outfit this time, Andy decided I needed a treat." She pulled open her phone and started flicking through to show us images of her current options.

Rachel leaned in and declared that she was going in her birthday suit, since absolutely nothing at home fit and she couldn't find anything that made her feel good.

"Well, if having it all hung out does make you feel good, then why not!" I stifled a giggle as Talia bellowed.

"Well, if any of us get desperate for a wee on the walk back to mine, at least we'll have a bush to hide behind!" Tina said and I snorted as I took a sip of coffee.

Holly softly chuckled to herself at the back and shook her head, "Honest, I've never met a bunch as crazy as you."

The team did a great job of distracting me from the news that today was my review day, but I couldn't help but worry that maybe Dr Cook might have said something to Dr Reeve about my competence, or rather perceived incompetence. What if I had failed my probation period? Was I going to be fired? Was the awkwardness between Nick and I going to cost me my job?

A buzz on my phone signalled a text arrival – Nick was on his way back to the practice. I finished the discharge I was working on, hands shaking as I tried to type, and logged off before heading to the bathroom and then downstairs to see if he had arrived yet.

The inside of my chest ached as my heart tried to punch its way through, anxiety dripping cold down my arms and legs, and the effort to walk through reception, I could only liken to wading through treacle. I had never experienced feeling like this, my entire body a demonstration piece for the internal struggle, and all I wanted to do was leave. Surely it wasn't normal to feel like this at work?

"Josie!" A voice cut through and I jumped, the coffee in the mug I'd carried down sloshing to the side. "I haven't seen you in weeks, thought I'd imagined you! It's me – James!"

I almost didn't recognise him – so incredibly different from the scruffy, unshaven man that had introduced himself weeks ago after my presentation. Suited and booted, although jacketless, with his crisp white shirt sleeves rolled up neatly to his elbows, glasses teetering dangerously on the end of his nose. For a moment I was tempted to push them back up, but his finger had gotten there before me, and deep brown eyes came into focus behind his lenses.

"Hi James!" I smiled as I took in his appearance, and he stepped forward and frowned when he looked at me.

"Something isn't right – what has happened?" He said, a little too loudly. "Are you alright?" And, as if by invitation, I felt my eyes smarting and the waterworks whirr into action.

"I'm fine James, honest." I stuttered through and steeled myself against the roaring riptide of emotion threatening to drag me out the office.

"Come with me," He gently put his hand on my elbow and guided me out of reception and down the corridor and I willingly let myself be led away from the curious glances, teeth still clenched together. He opened consulting room nine and guided me inside.

"Sit." He said gently and I did not protest. "You don't look like the Josie I met a few weeks ago, what's happened?" He wheeled his chair to the one I had sat in and settled himself directly facing me; I had no escape.

"James, I don't really know you." I stated simply.

"Doesn't matter – I'm a good guy, I'm a doc, surely that makes me trustworthy!" He joked, his eyes twinkling at the edge of his gentle smile.

"No, sadly not." I lifted the edge of my mouth in a sad grin and shook my head.

"Which GP has you like this then?" He stated, leaning back, and running his fingers through his dark hair. I sucked in a breath in shock.

"Wh..what?"

"Well, if I'm not trustworthy cause I'm a doc, and you look like you've not slept in weeks and like a sneeze would knock you down – something must have gone on here. Some of this lot are dicks, I get it. I could probably guess which one, but I'll not do them a disservice, and let you tell me." He put his hand on my knee and the door, which apparently hadn't shut properly, swung open to reveal a furious Nick Reeve. The bang of the door against the wall made us jump and James snatched his hand from my knee and pushed his chair away from me hastily.

"Josie – I do believe you're late to our meeting." Nick said, not even looking at me as his gaze was too busy looking at James.

"Sorry Dr Reeve. Thanks, James." I scurried out past Nick, feeling slightly afraid I'd get burned from the heat of his fury, but James was clearly immune, throwing out a genuine smile as I slipped out.

"Ah, Nick. Sorry for keeping her." I heard Nick grunt in response, as I hurried away to his room, his footsteps soon following purposefully behind me. He pushed open the door and pulled the chair out roughly, pointing at the seat.

"Sit." It was a command, not a suggestion.

I shut the door and did as he asked, a little afraid for what he was about to say. There was a silence as he sat and put his head in his hands. The sound of cars passing outside, mindless chatter from passers-by and the distant beeping of a horn filtered through the open window and I waited patiently for him to speak.

"Right. So, we've got this review to do." He sighed and pulled his hands from his face, clicking the computer on. "How have things been?"

What? Business as usual? I stared, stunned by the sudden change in his manner. Anger dissipated, only to be replaced by an almost defeated expression.

"Josie?"

"Erm… yes they've been ok." I stammered. "I'm getting to know people now." He had pulled open a document and began to type.

"Anything you're concerned about?" He didn't even turn to look at me.

Lots of things. "No…nothing."

"Anything you feel you need support with?" His long white fingers danced across the keyboard, a shadow across his jaw indicating that he hadn't shaved.

"Not at the minute." *Liar.*

"Is there anything you particularly want to learn or any future plans for development?" He said, and I paused while I thought about it.

"I..." I took my eyes from his face and glanced at my fingers.

"Yes?" I felt him turn to look at me as his fingers clicked the keyboard.

"I'd like to sit in on a GP clinic and a nurse clinic if possible. I've spent some time with Holly, but I'd like to experience watching other colleagues consult too." The typing stopped.

"I...could arrange that. I suppose Jenny on the nursing team would be happy to have you, she trains lots of colleagues. As for a GP..." He paused looking at his screen.

"I think James would help me." I said quickly and his head snapped to mine.

"No." It was a firm answer with an undertone of warning. "You will sit with me."

"I...ok. Thanks, Dr Reeve." I nodded, not entirely dissatisfied with the response. I fidgeted with the edge of my skirt, pulling at a loose thread, and feeling very confused. I still had feelings for him, but he was acting so cold, and I just didn't feel emotionally insulated enough to deal with his freak weather.

"*Nick.* Why won't you call me Nick?"

"You're my boss." I said, not rudely.

"I think we've gone beyond the level of colleagues, haven't we?" He said quietly and leaned into me. I hesitated.

"I can't do this, Nick." His expression didn't change from that of entirely serious. "I don't get involved with married men. What's left on the review?"

"Josie, I'm-"

"I'm serious. Nothing more is going to happen." I said with finality. My heart sank, knowing that if he pushed me again, I would cave and jump him. I wanted to kiss along that rough jaw line. I wanted to take him in my arms and feel my heart heal as he buried his face into me. But I could not, would not, do that when his heart clearly belonged elsewhere. I only wished I could claim him as mine and have done with it. Why he was pursuing me when he had that beautiful woman at home, I couldn't fathom.

He paused, took a breath and said, "Ok. Well feedback has been positive. The team seem to be happy to have you. I'll organise for some shadowing sessions and that's all for now. Next review in 3 months. You

can go."

"Nick-" I said.

"Goodbye, Josie." His eyes remained focused on the screen, and I

stood, pushed the chair back into its space and left. This sucked...big time.

Chapter ELEVEN

Josie

"Come on JOSIE! Everyone is waiting for you!" A voice yelled and as I stood sharply, yanking my tights higher and higher, past even the heights of my belly button; I smacked my head on the toilet roll dispenser.

"OW! Shit! Ow! Guys wait!" I jumped and jumped, pulling and pulling until the crotch in my tights actually reached my own crotch and didn't swing between my thighs like a really unattractive hammock.

"The taxi is due any time! The others are waiting outside, darls. Are you nearly done?" Talia called from the bathroom doorway. The time for our night out had arrived and as it had been organised for a Friday, the girls had all stayed late and we had thrown ourselves together in the bathroom at work.

I was relieved that I'd painted my face on while the girls were using the cubicles, as all that was left to do now was yank on my favourite pair of black, heeled boots. I pulled up the zippers and stood and wiggled my bright, scarlet-red skater dress into position. The skirt of the dress swung lightly as I moved and the dip in the neckline teased a view of my chest that made me feel nervously sexy. I felt pretty awesome and ready to smash some moves on the dancefloor... although perhaps with some liquid courage to start.

"TAXI IS HERE! I'll delay them!" there was a shout from the door before it banged shut.

I swore and grabbed my bag as the cubicle door swung open, stashing a carrier bag with my work clothes into my locker, and flew out into the corridor, yelling, "I'm coming!! UGH!"

"What the-"

His jaw went slack. For not the first time, I had run straight into Nick Reeve and this time I had trodden on his foot. His eyes drank me in from my boot-clad feet to figure hugging dress and delicately painted face, his gaze almost hungry and I shivered in response; it wasn't cold.

"Sorry, I ... taxi. Hope your foot is ok."

"Josie, I-" He grasped my arm, but I brushed him off, determined that I couldn't ruin my night with the girls.

"Sorry Dr Reeve, I can't." I started to jog away down the corridor towards the stairs, dress swinging behind me and my feet wincing inside the boots.

"Nick." I heard him say quietly before I rounded the corner at the top of the stairs, not even turning back to look at where I knew he stood watching me leave him behind.

There was a cheer from the waiting taxi as I fell out of the door and into the car park, tripping my way across the pavement. I climbed in to see grinning faces.

"Bloody hell, she scrubs up well, our Jos." Tina said as I clipped my seatbelt in. "I feel like I applied my makeup with a trowel!" She pulled out several tins of pre-mixed vodka and passed them around. I downed mine quickly in a mixture of thirst and nerves as the taxi cruised towards town.

The sounds of laughter and gossiping consumed the taxi and before long I was caught up in a discussion about something to do with influencers and salaries, when the taxi pulled into the bay outside The Black Leaf Pub. We dismounted and tumbled into the bar, Holly buying the first round.

"You twisted my arm into coming here and I'm buying the first round as I'm not staying!" She yelled over the booming of the music.

"Bullshit!" Rachel said, "You're definitely staying and letting loose. Here's your gin, Josie." It had been a while since I had been out as my usual partner in crime had been unable to drink for so long, and as I grasped the glass from Rachel's hand, I thought of Rosie and the baby at home. I still hadn't been to visit but had made time for plenty of video calls. Rosie seemed to have taken to motherhood very well, and here was I, several years her senior and still out partying and single. I glanced into the gin glass and resisted the urge to lament my persistently single relationship status.

I suddenly felt a hand pull me onto the dancefloor, the bottom of my boots resisting my stumble due to the stickiness of the floor, undoubtedly due to the drunken spillage of many excessively sugary glasses of booze. The space in the bar was too small for the volume of the speakers, and my whole body trembled with every beat that dropped. Bodies moved in sync everywhere I looked, and I felt hips grind into me, sweaty arms brush past mine and faceless couples sink into each other as I was dragged by the hand through the parting crowd. The song was familiar.

'Talk dirty to me.'

I downed the drink in my hand and hastily plonked it on a nearby ledge as we passed, glancing ahead to see that it was Talia dragging me onto the dancefloor.

"You need to let loose! Shall we find you a man?" She shouted through the music, her eyes twinkling mischievously. "Ah, look... just what you need!"

We had just reached a small gap in the rippling mass of writhing bodies and my hips were swaying automatically with the music. Talia's beautifully coloured hair, purple with undertones of pink, complimented the beautiful, black playsuit she wore with a pair of silver stilettos. She pointed behind me to where Tina made her way through the crowd tentatively, holding a tray of shots and five additional glasses.

"Are you trying to kill me!" I yelled, but gratefully took a shot with the others that had just joined us and shuddered, replaced the glass and grabbed what looked to be gin. I knew I would regret only eating a rushed sandwich before allowing myself to be plied with alcohol, and though I also knew I would spend Saturday morning feeling sorry for myself, the thrum of the music down my legs and the euphoria as the bright lights swept across me back and forth in the darkness meant that nothing but then and there mattered.

I swayed in time with the music, feeling the buzz that came with the drinks, and suddenly thought of Nick Reeve. Nick and his bossiness. Nick and his bright blonde hair and deliciously charming blue eyes. Nick and his demands, his moods and his knicker-droppingly sexy smirk when he knew he'd got his way with you. *Why did he have to be taken?!*

Tina handed me another glass, but where had I put the last one? Was that Tina that gave me the glass? Where had she go- oh Talia. Talia was here now and there was a guy she was dancing with. His hands roamed as she moved around him and I couldn't bear to look because I suddenly wished it was me, and I needed a distraction.

"Holly…" I felt myself say. "Where's Holly?" But the voice didn't sound like it came from my mouth and the room was most definitely floating, even if my legs felt like lead anchors.

"I'm here, you're dancing with me!" Holly yelled at me, and her face came into soft focus. I hadn't noticed how pretty she was before, and the animal print wrap dress made her look like she had just stepped off a film set.

"Oh yes… you're beautiful!" I slurred and leaned into her. "You're a grrrreat pharmacist." I leaned my hands into her shoulders, and she laughed with a freedom I'd not seen in her before.

"Well, you're great too! I think the doctors will grow to love you!" She shouted over the music. "I know Nick has high hopes for you!"

I nodded and let go of her shoulders, willing my legs to move as I indicated I needed the bathroom. I staggered between smooching couples, silently fuming at their audacity to be so openly affectionate when sad singletons like me were around. My drunken heart ached, and I wished I could call him and make him come and dance with me. And suddenly the realisation that I had his number and that I *could* call him dawned, and I grinned to myself as I joined the queue at the bathroom.

"Josie?" He didn't even say hello after the line connected.

"Yes. Yes, its Josie. And you know you are a problem." I was going to tell him straight, he needed to know he was a problem.

"I am? Where are you? Josie, are you drunk?" He sounded concerned but I was *not concerned at all.*

"I am where I am!" I paused and winked at the girl looking curiously at me from ahead in the bathroom queue. "You ARE a problem because I can't STOP."

"Stop what? Josie where are you?" There was a clatter down the phone, and I heard keys jangling. The curious girl had very long eyelashes, I was sure they were fake.

"Thinking about you! It's a problem you know. Could cost me my job. Nah. But I have to go – toilet - pee. Stop being my problem!" I hung up and grinned at the eyelash girl. "I told him."

"JOSIE!" I swung around in shock, perhaps a little too fast as I started to fall, but James appeared out of seemingly nowhere and held my arms to stop me from dropping. "I didn't expect to see you here. Do you want a drink?"

"YES, I DO!" I left eyelash girl sniggering with her equally fake friend, who was particularly orange, even in the dark of the corridor just off the bar. I laughed out loud, "She's tangoed!"

"Are you pissed already? Excellent!" He laughed, his southern accent making him stand out in a very northern club. But I was too busy concentrating on keeping one foot in front of the other to notice if anyone had heard him. The song suddenly changed and there was a cheer as we reached the bar, James plonking a glass in front of me. "You look fantastic, Josie."

"Thanksss." I smiled and blushed as I took a large swig and grimaced, tasting Bacardi.

"I mean it. It's great to see you smiling again after the other day. And I want you to know... I'm into you." *Well, this was new.* He took the glass from my hand and put it back on the side of the bar and took my hands. "Actually, shall we go dance?"

"My drink…" Even drunk I wouldn't return and drink from an abandoned glass – my mother had taught me one thing in life.

"I'll buy you another after." He gave me a small smile and I felt his arm swoop around and a gentle push on the bottom of my back to encourage me to the dancefloor. We swayed and edged nearer to where I could see Tina and Holly dancing, Rachel taking photos of them with the faintest flash.

"James! Hi! Take a photo of us, will you?" And we dutifully posed, the girls gathering round me, though I couldn't tell you what expression I made for the flash, because I was having a hard time staying on my feet still, and it was taking what little concentration I had left. James must have seen I was struggling, for he slipped a strong arm under mine and pulled me close to let me lean, as he handed back Rachel's phone.

"Hiiiiii," I said languorously with a smile as my face hovered rather too close to his. We swayed for a time, the songs changing but our sway never detracting from our own tempo, determined only by my inability to hold myself up. I tried and failed to whisper, "I think I might be a little bit *too* drunk."

He laughed and I heard him tell the girls that he would get me home, clearly realising that dancing was now off the agenda. "BYEEE besties! Taxi for JOSIE!"

"Nearly there Josie, c'mon the door is here." James held me as I staggered about towards the pub exit. The cold November air was quite sobering as it hit me outside and instinctively, I grabbed for my purse to check I still had it.

"What are we doing?" I said to James, who pulled out his phone.

"Can you prop yourself up while I call us a taxi? You can stay at mine." He let go once he was sure I wouldn't fall, and I couldn't make the jumbled mess inside my head think clearly.

"James. I need to go home." The paving slabs on the ground were rippling and my stomach contorted as my vision swam. "Home please."

"It's ok you can come stay with me. Or I will come to yours. You need someone with you." He insisted as he tried another number, the engaged dial tone barely audible against the muted thuds coming from the pub windows. "I've left the guys inside; I should text them before I leave."

There was a sudden screech of tyres, which made the clubgoers milling about outside jump, and a black Lexus pulled along the cobbles and halted at the pavement next to us. The door swung open and out climbed a furious looking Nick Reeve, still dressed in his work attire, minus his jacket, his shirt unbuttoned and creased.

"Oh…" I breathed, and James frowned and quickly wrapped his arm around my shoulders possessively.

"Oh hey Nick… didn't think you were the partying kind of guy anymore. What are you doing here? We were just leaving." He said.

"I promised Josie that I'd give her a ride home. Now if you don't mind." He said and stepped forward, still avoiding looking at me. *How had he found me? What had I said on the phone?*

"Josie never told me about a planned ride home, now did you Jos?" He gripped my shoulder, not too tightly and looked at me with what I presumed was an expectant expression, but I couldn't tear my gaze from Nick's face.

"I… lift… yes. Erm, sorry Jamessss." I staggered forward and Nick reached out for me at the same time James moved to catch me.

"Josie, you don't need to go yet. We can get food and I'll get you home." James said hastily and frowned at Nick.

"Ja-" I began.

"You've done enough." His tone was a warning and James stepped back and walked away, my weight transferring into Nick's arms. He half carried me round to the passenger seat and clipped my seatbelt in.

"You shouldn't-" I began as he climbed in and the engine roared to life.

"No, I shouldn't but I just did. Where do you live?" He stated simply.

"Brands. Androth Drive. Number 17." I closed my eyes to quell the nausea which had worsened with the movement of the car. There was silence as he drove; nobody made effort to speak, and I was content to keep my mouth shut for fear of what might come out of it.

When I felt the car slow down fifteen minutes later, I opened my eyes to a familiar road and my house door looking all too welcoming. I glanced at Nick; my still very drunken brain unable to process how on earth I'd ended up in his car at my house.

"Is this yours?" I nodded and fumbled for my belt. "No. Don't move I'm coming round." He was at my side opening the door in a flash, and having managed to unclip my seatbelt, he half-lifted me out of the car.

"I'm fine. Honest." I insisted as we neared my door.

"I don't think so."

"You're a problem." I insisted, the alcohol talking again.

"Because you can't stop thinking about me?" He stopped me as we reached my door and turned his face down to mine, expression intense.

"How did you know what I was going to say?" I said to him, still very addled.

"Because I have the same problem." He frowned and reached round me for my bag to find my keys to unlock my door. He made it sound *so simple.* This gorgeous, *married* man.

"Why do you have to do this?" I huffed and brushed his arm off, wobbling through my front door that he had just opened, and ignoring the tilting of the world, I bent and unzipped my boots and kicked them off. "You just…You just…you're always there being gorgeously you. You're always there to tempt me. And now you're here. In my home. It's your fault I'm this drunk! I'm blaming you!" I ranted mindlessly, not even noticing what I was saying anymore. He had followed me into the hallway, shutting the door and he held my handbag quietly, staring at me with a dark expression as my inner drunk's voice grew steadily louder.

"You stand there, *staring at me.* You have the nerve to come on my night out and take me from MY friends and bring me home and stand there in MY hallway and frown at me. How can you? But you know what the biggest problem of all is? I WANT you. I want ALL of you. I can't stand here anymore and say NO! I can't-"

And before I could say what else I couldn't do, he had taken a stride towards me as my forgotten handbag dropped from his grip, pushed me into the wall and pressed his mouth onto mine, his hands on my neck and fingers entwined in my hair. He kissed me fiercely and with urgency, the roughness of his chin catching against my cheeks as he made his way kissing along the line of my jaw to my ear, where his heavy breathing tickled. My legs, already struggling, began to buckle.

"Say yes then…" He whispered and paused. I opened my mouth to speak but he pulled away and pressed a finger to my mouth. "But say it when you're sober. I'm not doing this now."

"But-"

"Goodnight, Josie." And, leaving me hanging in drunken disorientation and shock, he pulled open my front door and exited stage right. I groaned - tomorrow was going to be particularly unpleasant.

Chapter TWELVE

Josie

I awoke to parchment mouth and the ringing of my phone, which proceeded to turn itself off mid-call, presumably due to low battery. The weight on my stomach indicated the presence of a cat but only encouraged the sick feeling, and the inside of my head was probably as woolly as my hair.

"Uhh...." I moaned and sat up, Astrophe scarpering, feeling like the rising dead, duvet trying to claim me back into the grave. The clock on the wall read eleven and I froze. *Shit.* I was late. Very late. I was meant to be visiting the baby this morning and I had promised to be there at half ten. Argh, crap. I climbed out of bed and marvelled at myself in the mirror for a brief second. Knickers and bra in bed. Well of course, drunk me must've felt too tired to properly undress. As for brushing my teeth, *yack,* it felt like I'd gargled with something deceased. Last night's me mustn't have cared about personal hygiene at all and the clown in the mirror looking back at me was testament to the rush I must have been in to get to bed; the makeup was going to take me forever to remove.

I sat down to pee and sighed thinking of the girls. But where had they gone to? I frowned, Astrophe giving me disgraced stares from the bathroom doorway. Come to think of it, I didn't recall leaving them. I frowned in concentration... We were in the club dancing and then... No. Nothing! I thought harder as I made to wash my hands, even screwing up my face to concentrate. How the hell did I get home?

I rushed to my phone and plugged it in, urging it to charge faster and quickly pushing the 'on' button as it hit 2% battery on the screen. *C'mon....c'monnnnnn.*

Twenty-three missed calls. Fifteen text messages. My phone lit up as the influx of communications landed.

"Where are you?"

" What's happening?"

"Are you home? Call me."

My phone started to ring in my hand – it was Rosie. "Where the HELL are you?" She demanded and I winced.

"I'm sorry! I passed out at home, I got so drunk last night. Rosie – I don't even remember getting home! This has never happened before! What do I do?!" I sagged down onto the edge of my bed; phone still attached to the wire.

"What? Didn't you go stay at your friend's house who lives near town?" She said.

"Er…no! I'm at home, in my own house, with Astrophe."

"You don't remember anything?" She sounded perplexed. "Are you dressed! Christ, you don't think something happened, do you?"

"No, I'm in my underwear and my dress is on the floor next to the bed. I must have thrown it off. I'm going to have to call the girls to find out what happened. I'm never drinking again!" I whined.

"Yeah, yeah, you'll tell me anything. You looked good in the photos online, I love that colour dress on you. Anyway, right, we are going to the park. Get up, get showered and eat. I'll meet you at the park at 1 instead – usual spot." We said goodbye and hung up.

My phone started ringing again, "JOSIE! Are you ok?! Did James get you home?" It was Talia.

"Yes, I'm fine, what happened! James? Oh! James!" I suddenly remembered James buying me a drink. Oh god, I hope I hadn't disgraced myself. James must have taken me home.

"Can't you remember?" She laughed, "Oh we've been so worried. Are you alright though?"

I reassured her that my night had been uneventful and that yes, clearly James had got me home safely. I must thank him at work. I stood and made my bed, learning over with one hand as she wittered on about how much fun she had had, and complained that Rachel had tagged her in some shocking photos online.

"And there's one where I'm frowning, and you can see all my forehead lines! Anyway darls, I need to go text the others to confirm we can call off the manhunt. I'm glad you're ok! Love you." She clicked off and I sighed.

I had never drunk so much before, and it worried me that I had no memory of getting home, but I was comforted by the thought that it was likely James who had ensured my safety. The last few months had left me in some sort of confidence crisis, and now my emotions felt to be that out of control, I was beginning to wonder who or what exactly I wanted to be. Having left the comfort of community pharmacy, I almost felt like I was torn between wanting to prove myself as capable of more and wanting to work quietly and hide under the radar, doing the bare minimum to get by.

But it was not in my nature to remain under the radar, and just like I had pushed my team in community pharmacy to do all the services we could for patients, I wanted to be as good as, if not better than my colleagues so that I could pave the way for exciting developments. I wanted my team to be the best. I wanted to make my job exciting and new. But I just wasn't good enough yet, maybe I was expecting too much?

But my shoulders sank as I sat on the side of the bed and I sighed again with frustration, feeling like this identity crisis and lack of direction, coupled with this desperate feeling of loneliness that I had developed in recent months, were making me feel low. And maybe in my stupidity, I had gotten caught up in the heat of the dancefloor and tried to overcompensate with alcohol.

I shook my head, feeling Astrophe butting her head into my leg and leaned down to stroke her. "What do you think, bubba-girl? Am I silly? You bet ya, I am."

*   *   *

The sweet smell of fabric conditioner with subtle milky undertones that accompanied the peaceful, perfectly puckered expression and wrinkled grasp of baby Annie-Mae as she was laid in my arms had my ovaries in a foxtrot. She sighed with contentment, transitions of expression flickering across her face as she slept, with the barest hint of a smile.

We sat in the café in the park, the glass windows holding in the warmth but not holding back the threat the dark sky posed in the murky

November afternoon. Rosie looked positively shattered, her already-pale face almost translucent, and the dark circles hinting at the lack of sleep she was undoubtedly experiencing with a new baby. The perpetrator in question remained snuggly in my arms, tiny pink fingernails just visible and curled round the edge of a white crocheted blanket.

"She is undeniably beautiful, and I'm not saying that because I'm your bestie. You're amazing." I stroked her long fingers as Rosie sipped on a hot chocolate and sighed. "How are you finding it all?"

"She's amazing." Rosie sighed and gripped her mug tightly. I raised my eyebrows at her, knowing full well there was more to the story. "Ok, she is. But I'm knackered. My tits hurt, my belly sags, I haven't slept in weeks and while every piece of her is gloriously cute, I need a friggin' break. And you know what, I feel guilty for needing a rest. 'Cause what mother has a four-week-old and is craving a break? What mother sits their looking at their new born daughter, and asks for timeout?"

"Well. I ain't no mama yet, but I'm fairly sure every mother wants that. Newborns look pretty cute and snuggly, but I reckon they are a lot harder work than social media mothers make them look. Mate, I'll come round and sit with her so you can have some kip. How about this afternoon? I'll come back with you, you go nap and me and the little lady will get to know each other. I'll even order us pizza for tea later."

"My house-"

"I have seen before, and I honestly don't care what state it is in. If you're extra lucky, I might wash your dishes!" She paused and a silence settled over our little table as I took in more of the baby smell. I had learned from reading magazines that the one thing a new mother needs more than anything is a village, and I was going to be her village today.

"Are you sure?" She whispered, with tears in her eyes.

"*Yes.* I wouldn't offer if I didn't mean it. And anyway, it isn't an offer. It is happening!" She leaned forward and awkwardly embraced me in a hug round Annie-Mae.

"I honestly can't thank you enough!" She leaned back in her seat and dabbed at her eyes with a stray bib while I shushed her and gently rocked a stirring baby. "So, what's going on at work?"

"What isn't? I'm totally, madly crushing on the married guy, but I know I can't have him. And then there's the car-crash that is my job. I feel like most of the GPs just don't like me." The delicate eyes of the baby blinked open and for a moment I was lost in trying to make her smile.

"Jos, that really isn't the case at all. I mean of course you can't have married guy – but I doubt most of the GPs dislike you." She continued to try eke out more information about work, but I soon got tired of the negative chat, and we packaged up Annie-Mai into a little burrito of blankets inside the pram and headed out to the park and towards where the cars waited.

Chapter THIRTEEN

Josie

After a Friday night out on the razz, and a hungover Saturday spent with Annie-Mae and Rosie, I spent my Sunday pottering about the house, popping out only to call for groceries. Snuggling up with a book passed my Sunday evening away very peacefully, and I was grateful of the rest when Monday morning rudely came around.

At 7am I was already up, dressed and breakfasted, with still an hour to spare before I needed to set off. I debated with shoving something on the TV, but in the end gave up and decided to go in early and make a start.

When I pulled up in the carpark, there were only one or two other cars; the building was open, and I let myself in. It was still chilly, and my footsteps echoed as I climbed the stairs to the pharmacy office, opened the door and pushed up the thermostat. I fired up my computer, pulling my jacket tightly around me, and logged in to see a reasonable amount of a work. Come nine-o-clock, that workload was soon going to be unmanageable as the phone calls came in and the letters started being scanned on for processing.

I started looking through some tasks in the pharmacy inbox, assigning myself some to start with and processing one or two that didn't require contacting a patient. By 7.35am I was lost in a patient's record, looking for why they'd been started on a medicine several years ago, when there was a small knock on the door, and it slid open.

Nick Reeve himself came in with a frown, still in his coat, bag in his hand and his hair a little dishevelled. He plonked his bag on the table and my hand paused on the mouse, curious to see the intruder.

"You're early." He stated.

"I am."

"Are you recovered from your debauchery on Friday?" He said, an eyebrow raised and a mischievous twinkle in his eye. I felt a squeeze in my chest.

"I am." I narrowed my eyes with a smirk, "Why?"

"I didn't think heavy drinking would be your thing." He pulled his scarf from around his neck and bundled it up in his hands.

"I like to let my hair down occasionally. Maybe you should try it sometime." I leaned back in my chair, stretched, and stood. "Time for coffee."

"Ah, we don't tend to get invited to these social activities." He grabbed his bag and opened the door for me. I nodded in thanks.

"You don't need an invite, James turned up anyway. He was actually kind enough to take me home." I set off down the corridor, but his footsteps had stopped.

"H- home?"

I turned to see him standing looking confused, which was a first. "Yes, but embarrassingly enough I was really rather too drunk to remember. How chivalrous though, I must see if he is in today to thank him." Nick looked too stunned to speak, frowning slightly and almost a little lost. He gripped his bag with one hand, his other fumbling with his scarf. "Are you coming for coffee?"

"Yes." He followed me in silence, apparently thinking. But then- "You allowed yourself to be so drunk that you don't even remember being taken home?"

I stopped again halfway down the steps and turned, eyes ablaze with challenge, "Yes I did and while I appreciate it was a stupid thing to do, I don't appreciate being lectured as a grown woman, so don't even start."

"You could have been abducted or raped." He stated simply.

"I know."

"You could have been killed." He raised his voice.

"*I know.*" There was a silence while he collected himself and then overtook me on the steps down towards the kitchen. I scurried down the last few steps to catch up to him. "Are you done now?"

"Clearly you got home safe this time. Perhaps forgetting how you got into your home will teach you not to drink like a teenager discovering alcohol for the first time." He said curtly, completely unimpressed and striding through reception so fast I had to double my speed to keep up. I stopped by the kitchen, angry at being infantilised.

"I'm not a child you can chastise." I snapped.

"Stop acting like one then." He yanked open the door next to the clinical corridor and strode through without looking back, leaving it to slam behind him and the cupboards next to me, rattle.

"*Prick.*"

By 9am the team was fully assembled, and I was already 18 letters into my working day. I'd volunteered to take a shift on clearing some of the discharges, making sure that relevant monitoring had been arranged and that any new medicines or stopped medicines or doses changed of medicines were accurately reflected on the system. Sometimes I had to call patients to check if they had received a supply, sometimes I had to call the hospital to try clarifying something that wasn't clear at all, and other times I had to call community pharmacies to make sure they didn't give out old medicines and to update them on changes. It was all very busy and certainly took my mind off the morning's bitter exchange with Nick Reeve.

"I need an early lunch today, guys. The early start this morning has me hungry already." I offered to do the mid-morning coffee run so that I could steal biscuits from the kitchen, and popped downstairs to get the kettle on, where I happily bumped into James.

"Hey chump – how bad was the hangover?" He grinned.

"Oh man, I'm never drinking that much again…my stomach was not very happy with me all day on Saturday." He passed me the coffee, and I started to spoon it into mugs that I'd assembled onto the tray we used for transporting them upstairs. The kitchenette was in an open plan area of the reception offices with several windows, and doors nearby. I caught sight of Nick through the window into the admin room, he was standing by the photocopier with one hand on the machine, turned away talking to Gayle who sat at her computer. "I need to thank you though. You were amazing."

"Hey it was only a drink and a dance, it was great!" James passed me the milk.

"No – for the lift! I'm really sorry if I talked rubbish on the way back, I was so drunk I-" I broke off, catching a very odd look on his face as he shook his head. "What's up?"

"I didn't take you home." The grin slid from my face. "He did." My heart sank as I followed the direction of his eyes as they turned to look at the admin room. Almost as if he sensed us looking at him, Nick turned from Gayle to see us both staring and reactively frowned. My face fell in shame and embarrassment, and I sighed, my shoulders sagging.

"Oh crap."

"Sorry pal, he was in a bit of an arse, and I'd had too much to drink to drive you. Wouldn't let me get us a taxi. Not sure how he found us though?" He nudged me, and his voice dropped to a whisper while he grinned again, "Bit of a control freak, that one." He winked and patted me on the arm in consolation before wandering off with his coffee.

Nick had taken me home and I had totally blanked the whole thing, and then I had thrown it in his face when he came to check on me. I started throwing teabags violently into the remaining empty mugs, not really caring whether I got the girls' orders right. I was genuinely sick of the person I was turning into; this wasn't like me at all. This wasn't what I stood for, and this person inside didn't believe in drinking to the point of drop or getting emotional over the silly stuff, and I didn't entirely know if this instability was related to my stupid feelings or that I felt like in part, my relationship with some of my colleagues felt entirely toxic and unsupportive.

I put my hands on the counter and took some deep breaths. In. Out. In. Out. His footsteps sounded and I swivelled round to stop him and stumbled. "Nick." He paused at the door. "It was you – I'm sorry."

"It was nothing." He said flatly and pulled open the door, striding off down the corridor.

"It was everything." I whispered to the air, closing my eyes as the force of the door slamming on me for the second time today hurt my heart.

Chapter FOURTEEN

Josie

I woke early the next day feeling determined that I was going to put all this behind me. I was going to push through this overwhelming feeling of inadequacy and desire for Nick Reeve, and I was going to focus entirely on my job. And I knew exactly what I wanted to do.

I'd noticed an increasing pattern of patients who hadn't had their blood pressures checked, who were also taking blood pressure medicines, even some who hadn't had appropriate blood tests. Clearly the practice systems for recalling patients into the practice weren't working and lots of patients weren't having their health checked often enough. I was going to make it my mission to whip the practice into shape and get these patients seen. It was going to be quite the undertaking, all I needed was permission from the practice manager, and other colleagues on board.

I decided on a power-suit to get me in the mood for the day. Sizing myself up in the long bedroom mirror, I turned from side to side and nodded in satisfaction. High-waisted black trousers which made my waist feel smaller than it really was, with a floaty light-blue silk shirt tucked in that had a white laced floral pattern sewn into the collar. It was a beautiful outfit that I'd only worn once or twice, and it gave me a boost of confidence as I pulled on small black kitten heels, expecting to feel a satisfaction with delicate click with every step through the work corridors.

I painted eyeliner on like warpaint, guarding myself for the day ahead and dabbing a light shade of pink onto my lips. My face had always been plain, and the brown hair that had once been a short bob had now grown below my shoulders. I felt like I could carry the look of a stereotypical librarian. *Perhaps that would have been a less stressful career choice.*

"I'm putting this on for my benefit – nobody else's" I muttered to myself in the mirror, and with a 'meh' that sounded like an exclamation of disbelief, I caught sight of Astrophe jumping down off the bed and trotting out of the bedroom, and marvelled in the haughtiness with which she had held her tail.

When I reached the practice an hour early, I parked in my usual spot and did a final check of my face in the mirror. "You've got this," I said to my reflection and set off inside, not even bothering to get myself an early coffee, since I'd already been organised enough to bring my flask to work.

I set about logging on and finding the right screen I was looking for, not even bothering to switch the lights on in the room and enjoying the semi-darkness, a sliver of light sneaking through a gap in the blinds across the window. Deciding which patients to prioritise was going to be a challenge. I had the ability to use the clinical system to search patient records to identify patients based on predetermined characteristics, so I searched all patients with pre-diagnosed high blood pressure. I tapped my finger impatiently while the hourglass on screen rotated as it ran the search. Thousands, which I expected. I applied another filter to the search, identifying all patients who had high blood pressure, but their blood pressure had been checked more than a year ago. Hundreds! I pulled off the list and started working my way through to check my search was correct. Occasionally their blood pressure hadn't been entered correctly but typed freehand into the record, but it was going to take me a good couple of hours to go through the full list. Being an hour early meant I could get a head start.

"Gosh, is everything ok Josie?" Holly flicked the lights on as she opened the door and found me poring over a list of patient names that I had printed out, now with a large number of them highlighted, ticked or crossed out. "What's going on here?"

"I've had an idea, hear me out." I began to detail my plans for identifying patients who hadn't had appropriate monitoring, to bring them up to date, suggesting that we could use the support of community pharmacy if they were willing; their services allowed appropriate remuneration, so I couldn't see why not. I suggested we could then, having checked our existing patients with high blood pressure, extend it into a public health campaign to encourage other at-risk patients to get checked. I began to feel more and more excited the more I shared my plan, and I started brandishing the sheet of paper that listed the patients that hadn't been monitored.

"Did you wake up and the idea just came to you?!" Holly smiled, bemused.

"No, I think I've slowly created the idea. I really want to do it. Imagine how many patients we can get adequate control over their blood pressure and what impact that will have long term?" I almost wanted to jump up and down on the spot. "What do you think?" I waited for a moment, anxious that she would ridicule my idea, or slam it down as not worth the time.

"I think.... its brilliant. You need to pitch it to management and make sure you highlight that it will hit the funding points we need to achieve as well as all the patient benefits." She smiled broadly at me, and

I sighed in relief. "Now I'm going to get coffee, and I'm fairly sure you'll need a top-up too."

When she left on a coffee forage, Rachel walked in and caught me mid-excited wiggle in my seat, and I giggled when she raised her eyebrow. "Goooooooood morning dear lady!" I said.

"Well, this is an unexpected surprise, did you get out of bed on the excellent side today? Ooh and I love that blouse you're wearing; you look incredible." She shrugged off her jacket and hung it behind the door.

"I definitely did. I've got big plans, but I'll fill you in when the others arrive, so I don't have to repeat myself over and over." When Talia and Tina had arrived and my audience was complete, along with steaming fresh cup of coffee from Holly, I began to outline my plans to a captivated audience. Again, I brandished the list of patients, standing up to really drive home my determination to take on the project. I gave examples of recent patients who we had discovered inappropriately monitored as a team, inviting everyone to think of how many patients they'd seen that hadn't been checked. Holly told stories of patients she had seen in clinic recently who she had done spot checks on to find them significantly with high blood pressure.

"I'll of course need the go ahead from management, and I want training in manual blood pressure taking. But I feel like this is something I *need* to do ladies. I want to make a difference, no matter how small the results are and how big the undertaking might be. We might be the forgotten team in this practice but together, we can do it. Believe me, if this goes ahead, I've got bigger plans for after. What do you think?"

There was a silence after my speech and while Rachel sat open mouthed, Talia's eyes sparkled with her grin and she glanced at Tina who spoke first, "Bloody hell, who replaced Debbie Doubter with Darcie Driven, or is it Fiona Fearless?"

"I'm in." Talia clapped her hands together.

"Me too, lass. We can do it." Tina grinned.

"I already gave you my vote," Holly smiled, kindly.

"You totally amaze me, of course we can do this." Rachel nodded and stood to embrace me in a hug, which I accepted gratefully and caught the fresh smell of soap in her hair.

"Right, I'm putting a case together this evening." There was a collective giggle of excitement as we all set to work on the day's tasks and letters, but I couldn't keep this mounting giddiness building up inside.

I ate my lunch at my desk for the rest of the week, using the opportunity to put together a proposal with a fervour I'd not known before. I spoke to all the community pharmacies to check that they were signed up to provide the blood pressure service and had capacity to support, should my project go ahead. I kept the details under wraps though, only making general enquiries. I pulled off patient data to create charts detailing our most at risk and poorly monitored patients and I sought counsel from Rosie. Only she knew exactly what I had planned. I saw no doctors that week, and even Dr Cook's negative behaviour wasn't enough to stymie my progress.

By Friday afternoon, when all my team had left, I had a perfectly formed presentation which outlined a detailed plan for whipping the practice into shape. I had considered the additional burden of workload, relevant blood tests that might be needed (for this I'd worked with Holly, and she had given up her lunch to talk me through this).

In his absence from my day-to-day activities, my heart had sadly not grown less fond of Nick Reeve, and yet he had not sought me out and nor did I think he would after the way in which we had last parted.

"Josie?" A voice at the door threw me; Anne, our practice manager, came inside and pulled up the chair next to me. "I just wanted to have a chat, is that ok?"

"Oh, yes of course. Have I done something wrong?" Internally, I slapped myself. Always jumping to conclusions, thinking I've made some disastrous mistake or that I'm in trouble is one of my toxic traits.

"Oh, definitely not. I'm worried about you. We've not seen you in the staffroom and I've not seen you downstairs all week. You've been here early every day, and the last one to leave every evening. I'm not faulting your work at all, I just wanted to check in. I'm not the only one who has noticed, is all ok at home?" She said, worry written into her face.

I sighed with relief and smiled earnestly. "Yes. In fact, I'd been meaning to come and see you. I've been working on a project that I was hoping to pitch to you next week. I'm really excited about it, and I just needed the time in work to get it together."

"Oh this is *interesting*!" She grinned, "Is it too soon to do it now or would you rather come see me next week? I have a spare half hour, though I realise you're already off the clock."

I thought for a moment and my heart squeezed very hard and began to race. I was ready, wasn't I? The presentation was complete, and

I knew the plan inside out. Why delay? I grinned, nodded and, feeling the anticipation from the tips of my toes, "Let's do it now."

Chapter FIFTEEN

Josie

"So, in short, she's taking it to the partner's meeting on Monday morning – I think I smashed it!" I took Rosie's bag from her boot as she assembled the pram in the carpark, ready for us to take Annie-Mae into the library for a baby massage session.

"Of course, you did, o ye of little faith!" She unclipped the car seat from the back of the car as I held the door and then clipped a very awake little lady into the pram frame.

"Excuse me, as favourite Aunt I claim my right to drive the babe-mobile. Because, you are a babe, yes you are!" I wiggled Annie-Mae's hand and took control of the steering, stealing lots of smiles from my adopted niece as we made our way into the library to find the room that had been rented for the session.

"I have high hopes for this meeting that they're going to have. I reckon that you'll be in a management position before long." Rosie scanned her card at the turnstile, and I did the same in the wider entrance for the pram.

"Definitely not, I can barely manage my way through a bottle of wine these days, let alone an entire team of people." Rosie pointed to a door in the far corner, next to a sign which designated the area 'Junior Reading', and I navigated the pram through some narrow turns.

"But in time. I mean, maybe you'll manage another team in another practice? You need to have confidence in yourself! I'm telling you Josie; you can't let others make you feel less worthy of more senior roles." She followed my haphazard pram driving, muttering behind me as not to disturb any potential readers in a rather quiet library.

"Maybe. I just need to get through this and then maybe if it's successful, I'll be able to see myself as capable. Oh shit!" We had rounded a corner and caught a pram wheel on a revolving book display; it had destabilised and was about to topple. Rosie and I grabbed it together as it teetered dangerously away from us onto a patch of carpet and there were an almighty series of loud slapping noises as one-by-one, the books tumbled off the top shelf and landed in a pile on the carpet.

We glanced at each other and dissolved into a fit of silent giggles, and then a child's voice came filtering through some nearby bookshelves, "Look daddy, the lady knocked the books over!"

I knelt, just as a girl in blue dungarees came rushing round to start helping pick books up and my smile at her faltered when I suddenly realised that I recognised her as one of Nick's twin daughters.

"Ellie?" A male voice called, and I shivered in response to him.

"You should go find your daddy. Thanks for your help!" She smiled, looking at me curiously before running off. Rosie, who had been moving the pram to allow herself space to help with picking books up, touched my shoulder.

"You look like you've seen a ghost." She frowned and I passed her a few books from where I knelt on the floor.

"That's the girl from the park..." I looked at her conspiratorially.

"The twin? Oh...*his twins? The doctor?*" Her eyes widened and we started tidying books faster. Annie-Mae started to wail loudly as I realised some books had slid under the nearby shelving unit.

"I'm going to have to get her out of here, will you be ok meeting me in there?" Rosie said with a grimace, and I nodded, desperately grabbing the remaining books. I finished pushing the books onto the rotating shelf, ensuring the spines were all facing outward, and turned to make my way towards the baby massage class.

"You're Josie, aren't you?" I jumped, and my hand flew to my chest in shock, as I nearly ran into one of the twins.

"You must be Eva?" Pink jeans and a white top gave away that she wasn't her sister. I smiled and knelt to her height. "Did Ellie remember me from the park?"

"Yes. Will you read a story with me?" She showed me a book she was holding, her expression more reserved than her sisters had been. I was taken aback, the forthrightness of kids not failing to surprise me. Reading to her would have been my pleasure, only Rosie was waiting for me, and I was sure her father would have found fault with my giving in to her request.

"Eva, where are you?" Nick's voice preceded him as he rounded the corner and froze as he took in the sight of me kneeling next to his daughter. Ellie came rushing to join us.

"It *is* you!" She beamed, "Look daddy, it's your friend Josie!" He nodded at me from the corner of the bookshelf at the end of the row, seemingly unsure what to say. "Will you read us a story please? Daddy read us one, but we want another!" I looked at Nick.

The girls turned to look at him, Eva waving her book and Ellie bouncing excitedly. Rosie could wait for me; I'd send her a text and join her later in the class. I knew *I* wanted to read for them but I watched him toying with the idea, his brows knit with worry.

"Please daddy!" He looked from the girls to me.

"Do you...will you?" I nodded at him, "Ok then." The girls jumped with excitement and grabbed a hand of mine each, leading me past him. I gave him an encouraging smile and my chest fluttered excitedly as I caught the familiar smell of his aftershave. He seemed troubled...but not angry. I wondered if our last meet weighed on his mind, and the weight of our disagreement landed heavily in the pit of my stomach.

The girls led me to a clump of beanbags, and I settled myself into a large grey one, big enough for all three of us. Excusing myself to send a quick text message to Rosie, the girls joined me on either side and once the message was sent, I reached for the book that Eva still held in her hand.

"The Princess Who Made It Herself" I smiled as I read the title. *Of course, she did.* I began to read, using the best character voices I could muster, even bursting into a kind-of Shrek-style accent for one of the monsters that the Princess encountered along the way. The girls laughed, which only served to encourage me more, and by the end we were in all in fits of giggles as I did entirely the wrong accent for the wrong character, having become caught up in the story.

"The End." I had suspected Nick had vanished to wander round the library, but when I looked up from closing the book, he was leaning next to a nearby bookcase in the corner, a sad smile on his face as he watched us. Tall, broad, and handsome as ever, I ached for him. Our last kiss felt like a lifetime ago and I felt my resolve to forget my feelings weaken as our eyes met, and his expression for a split second, became one of hunger and desire.

"Again!" Ellie shouted, breaking the silence as Eva took the book and started to look at the pictures again.

"Sorry girls, that's all I have time for today! You might have to pull me out of the beanbag though, I think it's starting to eat my bum!" There was a giggle and they heaved me to my feet, pulling on my arms.

"Go choose your books to take home, girls." Nick ushered them away and turned to me, "Your Scottish accent is... questionable at best, Toyota. Good job they're not au fait with accents." He smirked, a mischievous look in his eye. I stuffed my hands into my pockets, suddenly a little nervous. Our last encounter at work had not been a pleasant one, and his disdain for me had hurt. I couldn't just forget it, no matter how much I currently craved him. But despite the protestations of my brain's logic, my body was giving away its yearning for him; my face flushed, and I lowered my eyes in embarrassment.

"I never professed to be an expert."

"No. But you've been awfully good at hiding this week." He said in an undertone. His smile vanished and he took a step towards me, reaching his hands out to slide gently under my arms onto my waist and pull me in. I stumbled forwards and my hands grasped his arms to steady myself. "Can we forget about it all?"

I was conflicted. I'd promised myself I'd not get involved but when things felt so good like this, how could I say no to him? But also, how could I override the terror that he was a married man, and risking it all with his children just several rows of books away? My heart thudded impatiently, my knees weak and my chest tight with panic, torn between my head and my heart.

"Daddy!" There was an excited squeal from two rows away and he let go of me in surprise and stepped back, looking around, all tension dissolved. My decision was made for me.

"I have to go Dr Reeve, I'm sorry. Tell the girls I enjoyed the story." The familiar empty ache in my chest returned as I hurried away from him and left him standing watching after me, the faint chatter of his girls a few rows down.

"Did he find you?" Rosie whispered as I settled down beside her and a wriggly Annie-Mae, pulling my jacket off and picking up a cushion. She looked at me as she rotated little baby legs, alongside the other parents and their babies in the circle on the carpeted floor.

I nodded but then shook my head, indicating I'd explain all later. A baby massage session was not the time to describe exactly how nothing had happened and yet I felt tattered and weather-beaten inside.

*   *   *

On Monday morning, I told the girls about how Anne was taking my presentation and project proposal to the partners' meeting, and I was heartened to see how excited they were for me. As lunch rolled by, the girls went to eat, but I was stuck with a particularly challenging patient scenario, and a phone call to the hospital left me on hold. It was only after the girls returned that I was able to break away for lunch, and I hurried along the corridor to the soundtrack of my own stomach grumbles, and into the staff room to heat up some soup.

"So, it seems you're making some plans up or other to get patients in." Dr Cook had followed me into the staff room, and I felt like I'd been dipped in ice when I heard him speak, tongue seeming to double in size as I turned to speak to him.

"Er… yes, I h-h-have." I prayed the microwave would cook my soup faster. He was a big man, his jam-jar style glasses sat precariously on the end of a wide nose. His pokey little eyes were unnaturally magnified and he surveyed me with distaste; my legs began to tremble with fear.

"And what is it exactly you hope to achieve?" He said rudely.

"I – I – I want to see the patients monitored better than we are doing." The microwave continued to hum behind me, and in an attempt to move further away from him, I had flattened myself against the counter. He didn't make to move nearer and there was considerable distance between us, but the fight or flight instinct had failed to do anything but leave me a deer in headlights.

"Look, I don't know who you think you are, but you have barely been here two minutes and have no authority to start pretending you know things, when in fact your knowledge is pitiful. Stop pretending to be something you clearly aren't." He spat. "The practice doesn't want you here, even more so now that you've actually shown up. Change isn't always for the better, this I have seen."

He left as the microwave pinged to completion, and with his exit James walked in looking concerned. "Are you alright?"

"Yes. No. No, definitely not." My legs were worse than unset jelly and he steered me to a seat before I spilled onto the floor. "Did you hear...?"

James shifted uncomfortably and went to the microwave to fetch my soup. "Erm, some. But don't worry it's just his nature to get stressed about things that are new."

"He... he said I'm not welcome." I pushed the soup away as he put it down at the table in front of me. My hands shook so I balled them into fists. I felt as though my insides were ready to become my outsides. I wanted to leave this practice and never return, feeling humiliated and ridiculous. How could he have spoken to me like that? How was it ok to suggest that I was not welcome, simply because I strove to do better? Was it my fault for seeming incapable? Did I show weakness? I felt ashamed of myself for thinking I could instigate change.

"Nah, I'm sure he didn't, are you sure you didn't mishear?" James shook his head and pushed the soup back towards me, now sitting opposite.

"No. He definitely said I wasn't wanted." I crossed my arms to hold myself, feeling in danger of falling apart.

"That doesn't seem right. Let me do some digging, ok? I'll find out what's going on." James leaned forward and squeezed my arm. "Do you fancy coming to mine on Friday? We could go see a movie – it might cheer you up."

"Sure… ok." I nodded, barely aware that he had gotten up and made to leave.

"It's a date." He said… and it didn't even register.

Chapter SIXTEEN

Josie

I didn't tell anyone else what had happened. I was frightened and scared, but most of all ashamed of being considered incapable. I climbed into my car on Monday evening, and it connected to the Bluetooth on my phone automatically, continuing that morning's song from my playlist, which suddenly hit different as I drove.

'You think the only people who are people...are the people who look and think like you. But if you walk the footsteps of a stranger...you'll learn things you never knew you never knew.'

I pulled up at the lights as they turned red, and a sob that I didn't know was there left my body. I slammed my hands hard onto the steering wheel and struggled to see from the tears gathering in my eyes.

"How high does the sycamore grow? If you cut it down, then you'll never know!" I yelled along to a song that I'd known from childhood. I felt splintered into a thousand tiny pieces. Perhaps I was being dramatic, but this was pain I'd never known before. Pain of rejection, of shame in not being enough despite trying my hardest. I had never been spoken to like that, nor had I ever been made to feel an outcast, unwanted or unwelcome.

When I arrived home, there were no tears left inside and my top was soaked to the skin. This man had single-handedly ruined my new start in general practice, and I couldn't do anything but blame myself for being incompetent, and for trying to be something that I was clearly not.

I laid awake all night, his words bouncing round and round my head. By morning, I was not only completely empty from having not eaten, but I was also a living zombie. I felt hollow and numb. There were several missed calls and texts from Rosie, ones I'd ignored because I didn't have heart to pretend that I was ok, nor tell her what had happened. The phone rang again as I was getting dressed, and I decided I'd best answer it before she sent the police to my house.

"Hullo."

"Where have you been?" She demanded at once. "Have you not seen my missed calls?" I took a deep breath and opened my mouth to speak… but nothing would come out. I feared if I spoke, then suddenly tears would arrive again, and with them an avalanche of sobs. "Josie?"

"I…I…." I started to pant, trying to stop the emotion in its tracks. I sucked in and blew out, one breath at a time.

"What on earth? Are you ok? Should I call the police?" She sounded panicked.

"No." I managed. "O....K. Wait." I panted a little bit again and she remained entirely silent as I carried the phone to the kitchen and poured myself a glass of water and took a sip. "Sorry."

"I'm here its ok." She waited.

"Yesterday...at work" I carried my glass to the sofa and plonked myself down, still in just shirt and knickers. "a doctor told me...he said...he said I need to leave."

"WHAT?"

"I'm not wanted. I'm not good enough." I closed my eyes, my chin wobbling and my teeth clenched together.

"That is the biggest load of horse-shit that I've ever heard in my life! Who was this? What did you say? Have you made a complaint?" I could hear the anger in her voice and picture the very expression she wore.

"Dr Cook. I've done nothing and I can't do anything. As a senior partner, he is one of the bosses. I think I'm going to call in sick." I grabbed for a tissue and dabbed at my eyes.

There was a pause on the line as she thought. "Ok, I'm going to need some time to process how to proceed with this. But first, you are going in to work."

"No." I said firmly.

"Yes, Josie. This man might be a GP, a partner, and a senior member of staff but through all of that, he is but just one thing: a bully. He's sore that a woman determined to make a success of her role has come into the practice, when he didn't want the funds used for your role in the first place. He's scared that you're about to show him just how much you can achieve, and in his fear that you will grow so tall you'll take the shine of the top off his head, he is cutting you down. And I will not stand back and let you accept being cut down when you are the most beautiful, the most creative and thoughtful, and the most determined flower that I ever did have the pleasure to work with. I will not let you wither at home Josie. You will suck it up and stand tall and you will go into work this week and do the job you were born to do. Do you hear me?"

"Y..y..yes." I shook with the tears again, desperately craving a hug.

"Do you have time for a shower before work?" She asked.

"Yes."

"Right then. Get up, get in the shower, and wash him out of your hair. Get out and get dressed in something that gives you confidence. Drink coffee, eat something nice and drive to that goddamned practice and bloom your petals all over to spite him. I hope he trips over his own abnormally large ego." She spat.

She *was* right, of course. But following her orders sounded so much harder than sitting on the sofa would be. And I was scared. I didn't feel strong enough to face him. As if she sensed my thought pattern, Rosie said quietly, "You are more than capable of this. I know you can do it. I'm at the end of the phone if you need me."

I thought for a moment, my finger rubbing its way around the top of my glass of water, causing an eerie note to ring out. If I stayed in the comfort of my home, it would only delay the inevitable of having to return, even if I resigned. And he would win. I couldn't let such an awful man make me feel like this. He might have knocked me down, but rather than stay down… was it possible I could get back up? I took a deep breath.

"I'll do it." I said resolutely.

"That's ma girl."

*   *   *

The rest of Tuesday was dreadful, and I was terrified that I might run into Dr Cook. I told no one at work what had happened, but after learning that he was now on annual leave for two weeks, I took the breathing room and used it to plough all my remaining energy into getting the blood pressure monitoring clinics set up. Anne had sent me an email with all the clinical teams cc'd in, detailing the response to my project presentation, and handing over all planning to me. The meeting had been a success, despite clear grievance on Dr Cook's part. I was so busy working with the reception manager to organise rotas for blood pressure checks, getting the community pharmacy teams on board, and planning follow up slots, that I barely had the time to focus on what had happened. Rosie was still stewing on what had happened to me and considering our next move. I didn't sleep well though, still pondering Dr Cook's words every night, and I woke early every day.

By the following Tuesday, at least a hundred patients had received text messages to arrange for monitoring and between the practice team and the community pharmacies, we were beginning to make a difference. I was tired, and therefore glad to have booked some hours off that afternoon, so that I'd be finishing early to go meet Rosie for coffee. As I climbed out of my car, on a very cold December morning, Nick pulled up in his Lexus. Snow was falling, but not settling, and there was a dusting on the roof of my car.

I drew my coat around me as I grabbed my bag from the back seat and by the time that I had shut the door, he was already by my side. "You've been hiding from me again."

"Big project." I said, my scarf muffling the sound.

"Ah yes, I have a couple of patients that I've seen in the last couple of days whose bloods have returned abnormal following your requests." I followed him to the door.

"That's good to know we are catching these people." I said as he held the door open for me after keying in the code. I dusted my coat down of snowflakes and he pulled my scarf gently away from my face to dust it down for me, his gaze dropping to my mouth before meeting my eyes.

"You're with me today." He stated simply.

"I am?"

"Yes, in clinic all morning. You wanted some time with a GP, did you not?" I nodded. "Then come down for 9am." We parted, him down the corridor and me up the stairs to the pharmacy office. I logged onto the computer, then left my bag and coat to go get coffee before making a start on some urgent letters. By ten to nine, the rest of the team had assembled, and I left them for the morning to go join Nick in his room.

"Come in." I heard him say after I knocked, and I pushed open the door. "Take a seat." He had pulled up a spare chair next to him so that I could sit and see his screen, and we spent a few minutes looking at his ledger for the day. He looked to a have a mixed clinic, with a mixture of young and old patients, some in person appointments, a house visit, and some telephone calls.

Our feelings were set aside, as the patients were the priority today and the morning clinic went ahead smoothly. With my notepad and pen, I made notes as he talked to patient after patient after patient, always taking the time to introduce me. It struck me how at ease he was with patients, playful with the children and chatty with the older ones. The patients clearly adored him, and I realised that I did too. My heart swelled with pride as I watched him wash his hands over the sink in preparedness for the next patient, and he raised his eyebrows in the mirror on the wall as he caught me staring at him.

"Something on your mind, Toyota?" He wore tight black trousers, as was his custom, and a navy shirt today. His hair was longer than I'd seen it, perhaps overdue for his usual trim, a fringe starting to curl onto his forehead. I blushed under the gaze of his reflection.

"I'm enjoying myself." I smiled and doodled on my notepad from my seat.

"Good. The next patient is a 6-week postnatal check. I'll check mum and baby." He left the room to call the patient in and a tall, thin brunette woman followed him back in, baby fast asleep in a wrap she was wearing.

"Morning doctor." She said and smiled at me curiously after greeting Nick. He introduced me and discussed with her the plan for the check.

"Now, Mrs Jones, while I'm doing your check, are you happy for Josie to hold baby?" The absence of pram or car seat meant that there was nowhere safe to lay baby while she had her examination. A flutter of excitement built up and I beamed as Mrs Jones carefully unwrapped the bundle and passed him to Nick, who then passed him to me. Our eyes met as I took the baby boy and I had to resist a sigh. Damn those ovaries of mine.

"He's beautiful Mrs Jones." I said as I bobbed him gently in my arms to settle him again. "How are you doing at home?" I asked. Nick examined her as she spoke to me about the sleep challenges she had been facing and we discussed everything from her mental health to nappies and milk.

When both mum and baby had been sufficiently examined and sent on their way, I reset the room as he finished typing his notes. He leaned back and stretched, "Last patient of the morning done."

"That was brilliant. You're so good with them all!" I gushed, unashamed of giving him praise. "Thanks for this morning. I've learned a lot."

I moved my chair back to the corner of his room, and he swung his chair round to assess me as I collected my notepad. "You look tired."

"I'm fine. But I do have a question for you." I said, finally daring to ask a question that had been burning for weeks. "How did you know where to find me when we were out that night?"

"Your colleagues have a propensity to overshare on social media – they shared photos of you online and tagged their location. It did not take a stroke of genius to locate you." His eyes darkened as his gaze drank me in.

"Ah. I…er…did appreciate the lift. I'm sorry I forgot it was you. I hadn't meant to cause a problem." I fiddled with my pen.

"I do have a problem." He said darkly, and I glanced at him. "You're causing issues for me."

"What?!" I dropped my notepad in shock and retrieved it from the floor, did he know about Dr Cook? How could he know? Had James said something?

"I can't seem to concentrate as well on anything these days, and its entirely your fault. You're a distraction and somehow you keep managing to slip away from me." He frowned.

"Oh-"

"Do you still want me?" He asked and there was a silence while my internal monologue battled over how to respond. He stood and crossed the room, taking my notepad and pen and putting them on the bed before grasping my waist and pulling me into him, our bodies pressed together. His stubble grazed my neck, and he pulled my top to expose my shoulder and planted kisses in a delicate line. I shivered involuntarily. "Do you want...this?" He murmured into my ear. I breathed shakily, gripping his shirt tightly to steady me, and feeling the warmth of him on me.

"Yes."

There was a sudden knock at the door, and he cursed under his breath as we sprang apart. I exhaled slowly while he adjusted himself and turned to pick up my notepad and pen. He opened the door to find one of the nurses waiting, and he snapped at her, "What?"

She left quickly after a brief conversation, and he turned and started ripping an apron out of the wall-caddy in anger. "This isn't finished. Don't leave this room." He pulled a pair of gloves on and walked out. I stood, frozen. If he came back, I would give in and who knows what would happen. I wanted, craved nothing more than right at that moment to sink into kissing him again, but it contradicted everything that I stood for when he had family at home. I had to go and go quickly before he returned. Spotting the time on the clock, I realised my shift was over for the day anyway and I rushed upstairs to gather my things, still reeling from his touch.

Chapter SEVENTEEN

Josie

I received a text message as I pulled up at the coffee shop. *'Do I have to slash your tyres to keep you here, Toyota?'* I frowned as I debated whether to reply, but a knock on the window made me jump. Rosie stood expectantly waiting.

"What…no baby?" I said, looking to see if she had forgotten her sidekick as I climbed out of the car.

"Nope. Mike is catching up on daddy time, he's been working a lot this week and I was quite content for some me time. I expressed extra this week so there's plenty of milk to keep her from missing her human tap." She looked different, somehow. Lighter, without a pram and bags weighing her down. Her hair swished in waves down her back as she moved, and there was a hint of makeup on her eyes.

"You look lovely. I mean you always do…but today you're glowing." I pulled the door open, and she grinned as she walked past me.

"I wish I could say the same Jos, but you seem to look worse every time I see you. That place seems to be slowly wearing you away. You've lost weight as well, are you sure you're eating ok?" She grabbed a menu off a nearby table and thrust it into my hand, "Pick something calorific."

We snuggled next to each other on a sofa right at the back of the shop, ignoring the numerous tables which would have provided a more sensible place to eat. Two hot chocolates were deposited on the small table at our feet, with no expense spared and extra cream and marshmallows.

"Go on then…" She said, patting my knee.

"What?" I took a sip of my drink, feigning a lack of comprehension of what she wanted to know. She nudged me and my mouth sank further into the hot chocolate than I had been prepared and I turned to look at her in shock, with a creamy moustache.

"HA! I need a picture of that!" And before I could protest, she had snapped one of me, which would no doubt end up online later that day. "You know what I want to know. I got a text from you this morning saying you were in clinic with Dr Hot-Stuff."

"Dr Married Hot-Stuff." I pointed out after tidying my tash. "And he was perfectly professional and lovely…until the last patient of the clinic left, and he decided he was going to attempt to ravage me against his consulting bed."

Rosie, having just taken a sip of hot chocolate, began to choke on her drink and I laughed at how ridiculously unfunny, but simultaneously hilarious my situation at work was right now. "Please tell me you're serious. Because if you're serious, this is like living in a rom-com and I am HERE for it."

"I'm serious. We didn't quite get to the ravaging though... saved by a knock at the door." I took another drink and a waiter that looked young enough to be my son deposited our plates in front of us.

"Saved? I wouldn't call that saved. I'd call that a shame." She pulled a double cheeseburger, with zero salad and fries towards her. "What did he say?"

"He asked if I still wanted him." Her eyes widened as she took a bite of burger. "And in my total stupidity I said yes..."

She wiggled in excitement as she chewed on the burger, and I began hacking at a loaded baked potato. We ate in amicable silence until her burger was demolished and then she launched phase two of her interrogation. "So why don't you just ask him if he's married?"

"Because the last time I mentioned a wife, he looked like I'd slapped him." We mused for a while about his wife before Rosie pressed me for more details on our brief encounter in his room. I marvelled in his ability to unravel me, and for a moment imagined him totally unravelled himself, his shirt discarded, and all thoughts of gentlemanliness clean out of the window.

My eyes glassed over, and Rosie giggled. "Should I give you and your thoughts some privacy? Cause what crossed your mind then was most definitely X-rated."

"No comment." Her eyebrows raised and I shook my head with a small smile, feeling my cheeks turn red.

"You sly dog."

* * *

For the next two days, I managed to avoid Nick, having been reliably informed by Holly that he was working remotely as his kids were sick. By Friday, however, I was very much aware he was in practice from the moment I pulled up Terry and spotted his Lexus. He sent a few queries directly to me throughout the day, rather than to the pharmacy box, and I knew he was doing it on purpose to provoke interaction.

At 11.30am, Holly called for us to finish our tasks as soon as possible and then go grab a drink. "I've taken the liberty, in honour of FIF, to order us a delivery of pizza, and we are going to have a meeting together over lunch. Dr Reeve wants to come and sit with us all too. It was like a lead balloon had just dropped into my stomach and I swallowed.

"I brought us some posh fizz for today, it's in the staff room fridge – I'll go get it." I said, hurrying to complete my latest task.

"Are we getting smashed?!" Tina asked excitedly and I shook my head.

"Alcohol-free I'm afraid."

"Disappointing, bub." She tutted and I chuckled as I left the room. I'd need to get the cups from downstairs, but figured I'd grab the bottles first. I set off up the corridor, my dress swishing against my legs as I walked. What on earth did Nick want to join us for? I was going to have to act natural but being around him did things to me that made it feel impossible to act naturally at all. I sighed quietly as I passed the bathrooms.

"It's utterly ridiculous, Nick. The pharmacy team have been distracted by this stupid scheme and now I'm finding myself having to do more discharges." I froze as Dr Cook's voice filtered out of the staffroom; the door ajar.

"Look, it's not for long Giles. The project is only running for a short time and then they'll be back on full steam ahead." Nick spoke.

I remained frozen in the corridor, wanting to leave just as much as I wanted to stay and hear what they had to say. I flattened myself against the wall.

"I won't stand for it again. Take them to hand, it's a hare-brained scheme and I'm not nearly paid enough to put up with the volume of work that I do already without extra pressure. You're looking a bit shit, Nicholas." I leaned forward slightly, catching sight of Dr Cook assessing Nick.

Admittedly, he didn't look his usual self. His chin bristled with stubble, and there were some lines of exhaustion in his face. "You look like you need to get yourself laid. That's the expression of a man given mischief by a woman, I've seen it on myself" He laughed despite himself, and Nick smiled politely in response.

"Ah, it isn't that simple..." He shook his head.

"Women never are..." Dr Cook clapped his hand onto Nick's shoulder, and I cringed while still holding my breath. "I'm sure she's worth the grey hairs eh, Reeve? Those girls of yours are spit of *her,* aren't they?"

"She is....and yes, they are." He frowned, clearly uncomfortable by the conversation. I suddenly set off running in the opposite direction, deciding I'd heard quite enough and that I'd grab the cups first, my heart thudding fast and my mind on overdrive.

I finally had the low down and it didn't make for easy listening. Clearly, he was still married, and his daughters looked just like her. There couldn't be any other possible explanation for the conversation I had just overheard. My palms sweaty and my throat tight, I made my way downstairs to the kitchenette.

"You ready for tonight, Josie?" James caught me in my rush to the downstairs cupboards, looking unusually smart in chinos and a blue shirt.

"Tonight?" I said, confused.

"Don't tell me you forgot our date?" He put his hand to his chest in mock outrage.

"Date? What?" I smiled, embarrassed at having no recollection.

"I'm taking you on a date tonight…you said you'd go out with me to the cinema? Oh man sorry…well do you still fancy it?" He flashed me a grin and I agreed to join him, having no other plans.

"As friends though…right?" I said awkwardly, glancing to see his reaction. I was not prepared to complicate my situation further. He frowned for a moment, but it passed quickly and transformed into a huge lopsided grin.

"Yeah, ok." He left for clinic shortly after, and my thoughts soon resumed their post-mortem of the conversation between Nick and Dr Cook. I lined glasses up on a tray I found in the cupboard, huffing at Dr Cook's words, *'You need to get yourself laid'*. Did this mean that Nick was having problems in his marriage, and was seeking... solace? I thought of Cook and his chuckle and gave an involuntary shudder, finding the man entirely repulsive in attitude. I don't know how Nick found it possible to even pretend to be friendly to him, surely, he didn't really like this man?

"No-secco all round!" I declared when I returned to the pharmacy room with the bottles, having secured them after delivering the glasses, relieved that I'd not encountered further private conversation.

"Yes! Well, I'm ready...get pouring lass. Holly's just gone down to collect the pizzas from the delivery guy." Tina hollered as she pulled up a chair to the unused desks that had been fashioned into a meeting table for us all. Talia, looking every bit a siren today, swept about the desk distributing glasses, and I followed her round pouring the alcohol-free fizz while Rachel deposited napkins on the table by each chair. The door swung open as we all took our seats, and both Nick and Holly came in laden with pizza boxes.

"There's a selection to choose from, if we distribute them across the table then just help yourselves." There was a smattering of thanks as we all dove in. Nick attempted to catch my eye, but I looked away and struck up a conversation with Talia about her eyelashes, which were beautifully curled and with a hint of colour. She was naturally pretty, and as always, I envied her. Pangs of self-consciousness gnawed at me, and even though I was beyond the point of angry and confused at Nick, I still questioned why a man like him would even take one look at me when he had this beauty sitting next to me, under his nose the whole time. I marvelled in the collective beauty of the team, suddenly feeling like the odd one out, the dud of the group.

"Carry on eating everyone, I don't want to encroach on your lunch too much, but I couldn't pass up on the opportunity to grab your attention all together to pass on some information. As you all know and have been working very hard at supporting, we began running hypertension-specific monitoring clinics based on a project proposal by Josie." Nick nodded and smiled in my direction. I nodded and glanced at my feet. Talia nudged me, and on my other side Tina tapped my leg encouragingly. "Well, our initial findings show that we have fifteen new patients who have been identified as having high blood pressure and are now being managed appropriately. We have fifty patients who have now had appropriate bloods with pre-existing diagnosis and of those, five were identified with concerns and subsequently are having continued care."

I continued to stare at my feet, delighted to hear the project was going well, even in such early days. "One of our patients has written to the practice to thank Josie for personally calling her, since she did not have access to our text messaging system, and identifying that her dizziness might have been related to over-treatment. She is now taking less meds and is finding life much easier."

I looked up in surprise, knowing exactly which patient he referred to, and felt like the work had been worth it just for her alone. *This* is why I do my job. A warmth spread outwards, and I felt something new, something like pride and happiness, reach the tips of my fingers and toes.

"I wanted to thank you all, yes particularly Josie, but because you've all had a part to play in inviting patients and getting the clinics filled and the patient reviews done. This is amazing work and I'm so proud of you *all."* He emphasised his last word, and I looked up to find his eyes on me.

"This is bloody amazing!" said Tina, "See Josie, look at what you've done!" A small round of applause started around the table, and I felt suddenly obligated to speak.

"I... I'm just so grateful that you guys went with the plan and brought it all together. It is simple work really and I'm really excited to see what happens in the next month. Thank you so much."

"A toast then, eh?" Rachel lifted her glass and there was a chuckle. "To Josie and to us." Tumbler glasses full of pop chinked together in the middle of the table as *'To Josie and to us'* echoed Rachel. I lifted mine and remained silent, grinning at them all, and yet avoiding Nick's gaze, which I felt sure was trained on me.

"Right, you lazy lot, work time!" Tina called and we grumbled as we collected the rubbish up and Nick stood.

"I have to go back to work too, thanks ladies." Nick turned with his handle on the door, gave me a meaningful look and then left, leaving me as always with questions unanswered.

Chapter EIGHTEEN

Josie

By the time Friday evening had caught up with me, James was knocking on the pharmacy room door, demanding to know if I was ready to go. I looked down at my dress in dismay, feeling underdressed and ill-prepared for an evening out.

"You'd look great in a bin-bag, don't fret." James attempted to appease me when I moaned. "And don't worry about your car, I can bring you back here tonight - or tomorrow morning, if we end up at mine."

I raised my eyebrows in challenge as we exited the staff door, and he winked knowing he was pushing his luck. "Where is your car?" I asked. And he pointed to the far corner of the car park. "Oh, hell no."

"There you go!" He grabbed my hand as I took a step back, taking in the size of the motorbike. "Don't look so scared, it's an adventure."

"James, I am in a dress. Everybody is gonna see my ass." I tugged at the back of my dress with my free hand.

"Hey, maybe it'll free up traffic for us as they stop to look, can't be a bad thing surely?" He burst into laughter at the fresh horror on my face, and said, "I'm only joking, that's mine." His car was a blue Astra. He held the passenger door open for me, tipping an invisible hat, "m'lady".

I buckled myself in as he settled himself into the driver's seat, and the engine fired to life, "Are we seeing a movie first?"

"What do you think? Are you hungry enough to eat first?" He pulled the car out of the space.

"In all honesty, not yet... I had pizza for lunch."

My expectations for the evening hadn't been high, but James had pulled it out of the bag and surprised me. It was relatively easy to be around him. There were no obligations on my part, and he had me laughing with his impressions of the genuinely terrible rom-com actors we had just been to see.

"I chose it because I thought that you'd be into it!" He insisted, "Annnnd you still managed to cry. Win-win."

"Methinks the gentleman doth protesteth too much. You love a romcom, you just needed someone to come with you to make you look less sad." He feigned a look of hurt, and I poked him playfully, suddenly aware that I was stepping into flirting territory, and this was dangerous.

"Yes ok. I am comfortable enough in my masculinity to admit to loving a good romance film... sometimes I even shed a tear and need a cuddle for comfort." He leaned into me in the restaurant booth we had eaten in, and I smiled. "Have you had a good evening?"

"Yeah, it's been great. Just what I needed."

"Do you want to come back for…for a drink at mine?" He asked, a smile playing about his lips. I *liked* James but that's where it had to end, I didn't want him to feel like things were going to go anywhere. I thought of Nick, pangs of longing finalising my decision.

"Hmm. I mean this in the nicest possible way… but I need to go home. I really have had fun though." His disappointment was fleeting, but we finished the meal and he drove me back to my car, still ribbing me at the tears I managed to shed at the end of the movie, despite the terrible review we both gave it.

"You might change your mind you know." He said as he opened my car door for me to climb in. "On our next date."

"James…" I warned.

"I know… but I'm not going anywhere and if friendship works then I'm here for that too." He shut my door with a sly smile and left to get in his own car. I started my engine and sighed, feeling that things in my life were already complicated enough without James' feelings creeping in.

*   *   *

On Monday, I headed down to the kitchenette to make the drinks mid-morning. It was long past my turn to make them, and I had insisted without much resistance from the team. My morning had been so far consumed with clinic letters, lots of them from either dermatology or dietetics, with recommendations for prescribing various creams or nutritional support drinks.

Nick was in Anne's office as I made my way past with the tray of mugs, and as I deposited teabags into each one, James came bounding through the door, wrapping his arm around my shoulder, and giving me a squeeze.

"Jesus, you made me jump!" I laughed.

"Have you quite recovered?" He asked me, leaning past me for a tea bag and not caring that he grazed my chest in doing so. I frowned a little, this was more than I was comfortable with.

"From..?"

"From your emotional response to such a...what did we call it...dull and boring movie?" He laughed and I nudged him to stop being a tease, "I had a great time...send me your free dates via text and I'll whisk you out again." He filled his mug with water from the cistern tap, winked and disappeared out of the door.

"Men." I muttered, shaking my head. I picked up the tray of full drinks and turned to catch sight of Nick by the photocopier, an icy expression on his face which told me he had heard my interaction with James and drawn his own conclusions. Quite frankly, he had a lot to hide and no room to query my social activities. I was, after all, a free woman.

That afternoon, I found myself wandering back downstairs in search of a folder with measurement charts in for stockings. In the stairwell, Dr Cook rounded the corner and immediately rounded on me.

"I see you're still persistently meddling." He spoke quietly with a hint of malice, and I froze halfway down the steps. "You booked a patient onto my on-call list this morning and you do not have neither the authority nor the right to interfere. How can you possibly know what is appropriate to go on my list?"

"Dr Cook-"

"No. Don't bother. You're costing me enough time and effort at the moment, and I'll be discussing with the partners about the end of your contract. I've had quite my fill of your fantastical ideas."

He stomped up past me and I took some deep breaths to steady myself, but not before James' face appeared around the corner, clearly having heard everything. I tried to swallow the tears down, but my throat felt to be closing up. How many times had I cried at work now? Surely this was truly how it felt to be bullied? Or was it a case of me being far too sensitive to his behaviour? I gripped the handrail tightly to steady myself and James approached up the steps.

"Look, just ignore him. He is full of hot air." He mumbled.

"James, I don't think that's normal. I've never ever been treated like that. Why should he get away with it?" I whispered, for it was all I could manage to get out.

"Look Josie, just leave it. Move on. You'll be better off if you just keep quiet. It's just in his nature." He ran a hand through his hair.

"I can't move on James. I can't just accept being spoken to like that; it hurts." The tears started to spill over onto my cheeks and my chest throbbed with the pain inside. I pulled my arms into myself.

"Move ON Josie. Stop creating an issue. You aren't going to win." He snapped, losing patience and I took a step back.

"I'm not creating the issue. He is. And it's clear whose side you're on." I retorted.

"Josie-"

"Don't bother!" I turned and rushed away, suddenly wishing again that I'd never taken this job at all.

Chapter NINETEEN

Josie

I didn't sleep all of Monday night and at 3am I texted Rosie to see if she was up with the baby. To my surprise she replied and rang me straight away, conversing in a whisper. I told her everything that had happened, whispering too as if my voice might disturb her attempts to feed Annie-Mae back to sleep. As I had expected, she was outraged, threatening to turn up at the practice later that morning.

"Look, this is outright bullying Josie. He is singling you out and making threats about your job when you've done nothing wrong at all." Her voice was getting beyond a whisper, and I heard her start shushing, clearly having disturbed the bundle in her arms. "It's disgusting behaviour – and for James to say that that's just in his nature to behave that way is no better. James should be solidly sticking up for you if he truly calls himself your friend."

"I know." I croaked. Astrophe had been with me all night, her weight solid on my knee as I sat, propped up in bed in the semi-darkness.

"You need to raise a complaint. I'm serious. If you want to do it in writing, I'm happy to help you compose a letter. For now, though, don't panic. Go get some sleep." She clicked off and I realised then that I was shaking. The thought of Dr Cook bothered me so much that my whole body responded, my heart raced and even in the cool of my bedroom, my palms sweated.

Astrophe shuffled from my knee, sensing my panic, and pawed her way gingerly up my body, settling on my chest and headbutting my chin. "Oh baby, can I stay home with you today?" I took the purrs as an affirmative and sighed with frustration, knowing hiding at home was most definitely not an option.

My alarm went off suddenly at 7am, and the pain from the claws that sank into my chest before a thud on the floor indicated that Astrophe had still been happily settled there until the shrill interruption. *Ugh.* I didn't feel it today at all. I was sluggish to get ready, throwing on trousers and one of my less favoured pink shirts.

"Good morning gorgeous." Rachel welcomed me in as I tramped in with one-minute until I was due to start. "Oh. That good, huh?"

I sat heavily and gave her a half-attempt at a smile. "Fan-fecking-tastic. I'm ecstatic to be here." She wore a brown, wool dress today with brown eyes and brown boots to match. She was every bit as put-together as I was a shambles.

"Oh dear. Are you going to spill?" But at that moment, both Talia and Tina burst through the door, Holly following suit.

"Maybe another time." I said in an undertone. The morning passed fairly smoothly, and it hit me just how competent I had become in the few months that I'd been working there. I knew I had a lot still to learn, but I admitted to myself that it did feel good to be able to get on with work mostly independently.

At 10am, I found myself on the receiving end of a patient's yells, having to hold the receiver away from my ear slightly as to avoid discomfort. "I'm TELLING YOU the pharmacy wouldn't release my prescription because YOU dated it for next week and I need it NOW!" The girls took a moment to glance round at me, the shouts clearly audible around the room. There were a few raised eyebrows.

It took ten minutes of negotiation before we reached an agreement and an understanding, and I gratefully accepted a mug of coffee from Rachel, who had been this morning's barista. I took a sip and sighed, pulling off my headphones to have a breather.

"Sounds like you drew the short straw this morning." Tina said as she leaned over Talia to offer me a biscuit.

"Ah, she was ok once I discussed things with her and she realised she had another strip of meds in her other bag." There was a collective groan and the conversation turned to the frequency with which we were complained at, but it often related to medicines that had made their way into a handbag, or another drawer, or in the car.

"I can't understand why they think its ok to get so irate with us when we can see exactly how many drugs we issued and exactly when we issued them!" Talia said.

"I think it's more frustration at an overrun healthcare system and at a lack of individualised care and it just boils over, and we are the ones that get burnt." I said, "It *is* exhausting shouldering the blame for a system that doesn't work, and what they don't realise is that we take this abuse, call after call after call and we take it home with us, lay awake at night repeating conversations. All we can do is our best and when people appreciate that it isn't our incompetence, but a system-wide failure in care provision, then maybe they'll start to see that we are real people...just like them...and that we don't deserve their daily dose of abuse."

The girls had paused to listen to my exhausted speech, the phones beeping indicating callers on the lines, Talia's mouth had fallen open in surprise.

"What was that again...I'm writing it down. Our lass is the next Shakespeare." Tina had pulled open a pad of paper and grabbed a pen. "That was brilliant."

I blushed and Rachel swelled with pride, "I bloody love you. I'm so glad you're here." She leaned into me and squeezed, and the buzz of conversation resumed as telephones were answered. My moods at work seemed to swing dangerously between overwhelmingly happy and content, to desperately anxious and panicky. It was hard to know how I truly felt about work when it seemed impossible to maintain a continuation of feeling, and things kept happening to make me question my position in the practice.

I turned to the computer and chewed my lip as I considered the next patient and worked my way through the query. I called her to ask questions and find more out about why she wanted another inhaler, and it was clear very quickly that she needed assessment in practice, rather than just a reissue of an existing medicine. I steadily picked apart the query and raised my concerns with Holly, who agreed that she should go on the on-call ledger for the duty GP to see her. I looked at the appointment ledger, and my heart sank when I saw that Dr Cook was on-duty again. I'm not sure whether it was instinct or experience of his attitude, but I felt certain that he would find issue with me adding a patient to his call list, and not because of the patient but because it was me doing the booking. I began to shake involuntarily again, my fingers trembled as they danced over the keyboard, and my heart thumped strangely in my chest.

I wondered if he considered how he made me feel. Did he realise he reduced me down to a quivering wreck? Did he realise he made me feel undeserving of respect? Did he know just how much he scared me, and did he thrive off it? I paused typing and clenched my fists to still the tremble, taking slow breaths to calm the rising panic.

"Are you ok?" Rachel whispered.

"Yeah…yeah, I'm good." I smiled faintly. I finished booking the patient onto the ledger and pulled up the next task.

At lunch, I popped down to return a folder to the office, only to be accosted by the girls on front desk, Jess' hands pulling me across the office to an audience of curious glances and giggles.

"What? What's going on?" I gasped as I caught sight of a beautiful bouquet of flowers that was so delicately decorated, with sprays of gypsophila intertwined around yellow and red roses, and handtied with a rope bow. "What *is* this?"

"It's yours. Who is it from, Josie?" A crowd was gathering and beginning to twitter excitedly round me, the reception girls demanding their fair share of gossip. I fingered one of the roses, pulling on a leaf and frowned.

"Was there a note?" I asked Jess. She pointed to the small card that I hadn't spotted between the roses. There were only three words inscribed on it, *'Believe in yourself'*.

My heart stuttered and I clutched my chest, reminding myself not to cry. I didn't know who it was from but the timing of the note, given my anxieties of late, couldn't have been any better. Curious. Who *had* sent the note? I riffled through the branches, careful not to damage any flowers, to see if there was another note, even turning over the card in my hand to see if there was a signature.

"I have no idea who sent this." The note was taken from me and passed around for the examination of the rest of the gathered staff.

"Anne – look Josie has an admirer!" Shouted a voice. Anne, who had been leaving her office, mid-conversation with someone still inside, paused to look and her face broke into a grin.

"Look at that! Sorry Nick, I must have a nosy at this." She abandoned her conversation to join us, and I turned to show her the bouquet, "Goodness me, you sly dog. Who is the lucky chap?"

"Ah, I actually don't know." I blushed, then caught sight of Nick leaning, arms crossed, in Anne's doorway. I wobbled on the spot with the bouquet in my arms and Anne steadied me with a giggle that I'd never have imagined her capable of.

His frown, which I'd grown used to, was darker than I'd ever seen it. His eyes bore into mine with an intensity that triggered a shiver up my spine and while Anne's mouth was moving, I couldn't hear anything but the sound of my own heart beating in my ears. Clearly, it wasn't Nick who had sent the flowers, or why would he have cause to frown? I realised, with dismay, that there was a large part of me disappointed that he hadn't been the sender. This thing…this connection between us was undeniable and my attempts to ignore it were getting more futile by the day.

The crowd dispersed on Anne's orders, and I carried the flowers away and back up to the pharmacy office, to face yet another round of questioning by my own team. It took all afternoon of speculation between calls, but by 4pm I was glad that it was just Rachel and I that remained in the office.

An instant message popped up in the corner of my screen, *'Meeting next week – booking patients into my call list is not your prerogative and you've done quite enough now'*.

And in the few seconds I took to read Dr Cook's message and let it sink in, my body had already begun to respond. I could feel myself gathering sweat, ragged breaths came but the faster I breathed, the less oxygen I seemed to be gathering and suffocating panic began to rise inside. I balled my hands into fists and gritted my teeth, my chin quivering with the effort of trying not to cry. Never had a person upset me so, such that my entire body responded with a panic, and the world and its many stresses felt to be pressing in and consuming me.

"Josie? Is everything alright?" I felt Rachel's concern, though I couldn't make myself look at her. I couldn't speak, only admit that everything was very wrong indeed with a shake of the head. "Oh, Josie what's happened?"

I felt her join me, her arm wrapping round my tensed shoulders. "What's that? Why has he said that?" She was reading the instant message.

"I..I..." She pulled my drink towards me.

"Have a drink. You're safe here. It's going to be ok." It took several minutes of trying to gasp air into my lungs, shaky fingers holding the cup of water, and tears that were drying down my face, before I could eventually tell Rachel everything that had gone on with Dr Cook. From him telling me I wasn't welcome, to ignoring me, suggesting my incompetence, and threatening me with my job. I blurted it all out between body-shaking sobs and thankfully, Rachel had tissues that she passed me to contain the snot.

"Oh Josie. Why have you never said anything?" Through the blurriness of my eyes, I could see she was angry, her eyes returning to look at the screen message and grimacing.

"I didn't think you'd believe me, and I felt stupid." My body shook with a fresh round of sobs again and her arms held me tight. "I want to go home now."

I was still due to work another hour or two, but I had finally cracked. All the hurt that had built up inside about Dr Cook had broken out and I had no desire to remain in the building with the man that was making me feel this way.

"Josie, it's going to be ok, I promise. But yes, let's get you home. Let me sort something." She said.

"No! Please don't do anything." I grabbed her arm in fear, my eyes wide and face stained with tears.

"Ok. I won't. Let's get you to your car, are you ok driving home?" She helped me bundle my things together, held out my coat for me to shrug into, and passed me a tissue. I felt like a lost child being mothered, and her kindness reached me in ways that I was incapable of expressing, my throat clogged from all the crying. We descended the stairs to the carpark door in silence but for the clicking of our heels. I felt fragile, almost like another word from Dr Cook or anybody for that matter, might cause me to shatter into a thousand pieces. There was a part of me that wanted to be shattered, and blown away in a gust of wind, free to exist and free from worry. I was truly myself and not myself at all; I was sensitive, but I didn't usually feel so out of control.

"Josie?" I looked up to see Nick looking curiously at me from the bottom of the stairs and shook my head, concern evident in his expression. I had no time for any other feeling beyond this anxiety, this exhaustion, this emptiness that had settled inside after the tears had finished.

"I'm just taking Josie to her car; she isn't feeling well." Rachel said and they exchanged a look.

"Ok. Josie if you need me, you have my number." He said, and I nodded as I slid through the door that Rachel had opened, not trusting myself to open my mouth to speak. Rachel engulfed me in a hug when we reached the side of the car and I left without looking at the building, knowing that Nick was most certainly watching in the dark of the doorway.

Chapter TWENTY

Josie

On Wednesday morning I awoke in a state of confusion, having fallen asleep on the sofa. My coffee table was littered with an assortment of cups and glasses, and Astrophe was sniffing hopefully into a packet of half-eaten wine gums. I suspected from the look of disgust at the bag, and the warning whine she uttered as she hopped off the table, that I had forgotten to feed her last night.

I groaned at the pain in my back as I sat up and pushed myself upright off the sofa and trudged after Astrophe into the kitchen, where she sat flicking her tail expectantly.

"I'm sorry, I'm becoming a bit useless, aren't I?" I asked her in a croak as I reached for a tin of cat food out of the cupboard and peeled open the ring pull, tipping it into her bowl by the back door. I watched her begin to devour the meat, her jaw working overtime in her desperation to hoover the food up faster. For all the purrs and love she gave, I was simply her housekeeper and whatever Astrophe commanded, I was her willing servant. I watched her for a moment, avoiding thinking of painful things for a little while longer, but loathe as I was to remember the previous day, I had to confront it at some point.

Could I realistically continue to work in an environment that had me flipping between feeling loved and appreciated, and unwanted and disrespected? Could I live on the edge, waiting for Dr Cook to snap at me for asking a question? Could I live in fear? In my heart, I felt like *no* was the answer right there. I couldn't go to work every day not knowing how my day was going to end, fearing my colleagues, on top of the already demanding work with patients. I made myself a coffee, grabbing the glasses and mugs from the coffee table while the kettle boiled.

But could I leave behind Nick? Nick, who I barely knew at all but who had occupied my mind endlessly since the moment I had cursed at him in frustration, a need to kiss him firing up inside of me every time we found ourselves alone together, to touch him and to be held by him. It was a passion I had never experienced, a need I had never known I had. Nick... who didn't belong to me, but felt like he was mine, nonetheless.

My phone alarm signalled my usual time to get up and Astrophe, having eaten to her fill, rubbed her side into my bare leg in appreciation. I discarded my half-drunk coffee and bent to give her head scratches and she fell over herself in appreciation, giving a rare opportunity for belly rubs. I didn't push it though; an exposed belly wasn't an open invitation but a disguised trap for unsuspecting hands – overstay my welcome and her claws would make sure I knew about it.

"Do I go into work today then, lady-lou?" I asked her as I abandoned the fuss and went to find my phone to silence it, only to discover an unread text message on the screen. Seeing it was from Nick, I sank down into the sofa and clicked it open: *'She remembered who she was, and the game changed.'*

I sucked in a breath, recognising the quote instantly from Lalah Deliah, having treasured it from the book of quotes that I could see on my bookshelf from where I sat even at that moment. It was one of my favourites and had resonated with me when I first read it, but even more so now. *He knows.* My fingers shook as I stared at the phone screen. Would Rachel have told him? No. She said she wouldn't. Was he more perceptive than I usually gave men credit for?

If I admitted it to myself, the quote seemed to have stirred something inside me, and those feelings of needing to leave my job seemed to fade just a little, just enough to have me on my feet and heading to get dressed for work. I didn't feel strong, and I didn't feel capable, but the quote from Nick had done just enough to remind me that Dr Cook could not take anything from me, unless I allowed him to. He would only take away my confidence if I allowed him to make me feel weak; he would only take from me my joy if I allowed him to make me feel sad.

When I pulled up at work, it was with determination and a grit of the teeth. I had hollowed myself out yesterday and I was empty but for a small flame in the pit of my stomach that had ignited when I read the quote in Nick's text.

"Better?" A voice asked from behind me as I reached the top of the steps. I turned to see Nick himself looking up at me, unshaven and wearing a blue jumper and jeans.

"Um. A little. Thankyou." I felt the flame flicker and grow as I looked at him, the concern on his face obvious as he neared me, taking the steps three at a time, and reaching out with his hand to grasp my elbow.

"Are you sure?" He asked.

"I am now." I gave him a small smile.

"You will be." He assured me, his hand sliding up my arm to cup my face. For a moment there was only the sound of our breathing, a wordless exchange between us in which I tried to convey my feelings, my eyes unmoving from the connection with the blue of his, a rich and deep hue today in the shadows of the staircase. He looked tired again, and I lifted my hand to cover his on my face. He stepped closer and I basked in the smell of his aftershave, intoxicated by him, and still caught in his eyes. My lips parted, waiting for his to land as he leaned in, our exhausted bodies still sparking with desire, and I momentarily marvelled in his ability to soothe the emotional pain that still wracked my soul.

Before our lips could collide, a door banged along the corridor, and we sprang apart. Nick cleared his throat with a frustrated grunt, and I shrank back. There were footsteps in the corridor below and Nick stepped out of sight.

"Josie!" James appeared at the bottom of the stairs. "Did it work?"

"Did what work?" I called back, my eyes turning to Nick who ran his fingers through his hair in frustration.

"The flowers? Am I forgiven?" James called from the bottom and my eyes widened at Nick who raised his eyebrows at me.

"You…you sent the flowers?" I called, eyes still trained on the hidden figure of Nick, who frowned and shook his head with a sad smile, before pushing open the door behind him and walking away.

"Of course, who else could it have been? So do you forgive me?" James started to climb the stairs with a grin on his face, as Nick disappeared from my sight.

"Uh, yeah of course." I said, turning back to him. "Thank you they were beautiful." I didn't reveal that they were still in the pharmacy office, as I'd left them in my haste to get home yesterday.

"Are you...are you feeling alright about things?" He said, clearly treading carefully with his words. He stuffed his hands into his trouser pockets, and I noticed his long and narrow tie was crooked. He had a boyish quality to him, a charm I could see winning over lots of women, but I felt I could count him a decent friend, even if he wasn't great at tact.

"I'm not sure I'll ever 'be alright' with the way I've been treated. Whether I do something about it is another matter entirely." I smiled sadly.

The door behind me opened and Nick returned with a mug of coffee in his hands, nodded at me, as if it were his first time seeing me for the day, and he chose to ignore James entirely. I picked up a vibe, but James was unabashed and seemed not to notice.

"Josie."

"Dr Reeve." His eyes flashed at my formality, but he began his descent on the stairs. James sniggered silently and I frowned at him.

"I'm going home in an hour to work remotely. You have my number if you need anything." He said, and his voice vanished with him as he rounded the corner at the bottom of the steps.

"What is *with* you two?" I asked, identifying the animosity between them. James' smile faltered for a second, before it returned with a shake of the head.

"We just aren't friends." He shrugged.

"There's a difference between not being friends and being enemies. He seems to really dislike you." I started for the door and looked at James expectantly to follow.

"He knows I'm onto him and I see him for what he really is." He proffered. A knot of unease twisted in my gut, and I stopped outside the staffroom, feeling like I shouldn't ask the next question, and hearing myself ask it anyway.

"Why? What is he really?"

"Ah Josie, this isn't really something you should be hearing from me…" He paused and peered into the staffroom to check it was empty, pulling me inside. "But Reeve isn't the god he claims himself to be. He likes women, especially colleagues. I'm surprised he hasn't tried it on with you yet…" My face sagged in horror, a mortified blush creeping into my cheeks. "Oh Josie. Honestly, he isn't worth it. From what I overheard yesterday; he is as two-faced as it gets."

My mouth opened to ask again, mind too sluggish to protest, "Why?"

"He was talking to Cook in here, saying how you're needy and incapable of working independently. All tosh though, I wouldn't put stock in it." He laid his hand on my arm, once again my body shaking, though whether it was fear or anger this time I wasn't sure. "Josie, I'm only telling you, so you know to be on your guard with him, ok? Come here."

James wrapped his arms around me and pulled me into a hug. But I had frozen stiff and made no effort to return the gesture. My body appeared to have stopped functioning, while my mind attempted to rationalise why Nick had been heard saying such things. *Needy? Incapable of working independently.* But this was a training role, and I was learning on the job, or so I thought. I had given everything to this place, this team, and these patients and although unwilling, Nick had my heart too.

He'd taken it from me, used me and from what James had just said, openly criticised me in front of the colleague I had learned to dread. I had even built in a conditioned response to hearing his name, shaking, heart racing and sweating in fear. And the thought sickened me that I had thought myself falling for Nick, that I'd let him touch me and wanted him never to stop touching me. Suddenly the reservations I'd had about allowing things to go further had made sense, regardless of the existence of his marriage. Deep down I must have known what he was like.

I shuddered in James' arms, and he held me tighter, no doubt thinking I was enjoying the hug. I wasn't thinking of James though, I was thinking of my next move and certain that I needed to leave. Rosie would have me back, she hadn't even replaced me yet, and I would never leave her again. Lodging a formal complaint didn't feel like an option, for how could I lodge a complaint and risk being viewed as the incapable newcomer, living up to the reputation Cook and now Nick himself were making me out to be. And right at this moment in time, I really felt it: incapable and small, used and worthless. I had been stupid thinking I could ever do this job, that I could ever make something of myself. I screwed my eyes up tight against his shoulder, forcing myself not to cry because I didn't deserve even my own pity.

Sudden footsteps at the door had me flinging my eyes open, to catch Nick stumbling in with a mug. I felt James' head turn to him, keeping his arms firmly holding me, and Nick's expression darkened in scarcely contained fury.

"What are you doing, Cook?" Nick spoke slowly. *Cook?* I pulled away from James arms to look around for Dr Cook, but Nick was looking at James, who looked at me with a small, guilty smile.

"James?" I croaked.

"Nothing Reeve. I'm just checking in on my girl." He said, his eyes not moving from mine.

"You? Cook?" I breathed, lost.

"No, I'm James West, you've seen my ledgers."

"*Your* girl?" Nick raised his eyebrows, turning to me for answers.

"Cook?" I looked to Nick, still not quite understanding why Nick had referred to James as Cook, my heart cantering in my chest and finding myself struggling to draw in breaths. Nick returned to James.

"How is your dad, James? I've not seen him yet today, he's planning a holiday, isn't he?" He said without a hint of amusement.

"Your dad?" My voice cracked as I spoke to James, who looked at the floor, seemingly unable to face me.

"Yes. Dr Cook is my father. I took my mother's name." He sighed. I panted, the ragged breaths causing my chest to heave up and down.

I couldn't make words appear, my lips trying desperately to make the right shapes. I looked in disbelief between them, feeling like gravity was losing its grip on the floor and the sudden appearance of undulations in the tiles made it difficult to remain upright. What was this nonsense? Suddenly James' defence of Cook made sense and rage swelled inside of me unbidden, and I knew I could not remain in this room one second longer. I made for the door and Nick tried to stop me, but I pushed past, heading for the toilets, and locking myself in a cubicle.

I sat on a toilet lid, gritting my teeth while tensing my arms with anger, biting back a scream, and breathing heavily through my nose. Not one, but two liars. Two men I'd held in higher regard than they deserved.

I let my breaths slow with my heart rate, thinking of the number of times James had not taken the opportunity to reveal who his father was and had defended his behaviour. James had seen the impact his father was having on me and remained silent still. And I thought of Nick, who had seized an opportunity to tear James down at my expense. It was a very un-Nick-like move and though the truth was out, it was clear that Nick must have known about my anxieties with Dr Cook, and therefore Rachel must have spoken to him when I'd asked her not to. I was surrounded by people that I had thought I could trust, and each of them had failed me one-by-one.

I pulled my phone out of the bag that I'd dumped on the floor and made to call Rosie but slammed my thumb on it to stop the call before the first ring. I considered my options for a moment, bouncing between leaving immediately or handing in my resignation tomorrow and managing the last couple of weeks.

My eyes slid across the lino floor as I considered for a moment. No. I'd not give them the satisfaction of leaving immediately, people had lived through considerably worse, and I started the job, so I could at least manage to finish it. I wiped my face, shouldered my bag, and set off to the office with renewed determination.

*　　*　　*

When the end of the day loomed and Holly left with a wave and a week of annual leave ahead of her, only Rachel and I remained. I had focused on nothing but work all day, not partaking in idle chatter, nor asking any questions at all. It felt like I had tucked away my frustration to the side and while it was still there festering, I knew that my resignation would free me from this feeling of inadequacy, incompetency, and disappointment. Leaving would leave me free to be who I was anyway, without this feeling of failure or continuous desire to prove myself worthy.

Rain had begun tapping at the window and a cold wind was beginning to blow into the room. I heard Rachel get up and shut it as she packed up to leave.

"Josie, can we talk?" Rachel had logged off her computer, and it was time for me to do the same. I didn't answer but began gathering my things. I didn't really know what to say or how to say it. But she waited while I logged off.

"Sure."

"Something has happened, hasn't it? Are you going to talk to me?" She seemed hesitant, almost nervous to see how I would react.

"You told Nick what I said about Dr Cook?" Her eyes widened.

"Yes but-"

"And James is Dr Cook's son?" I said.

"He is. Josie I-"

"I'm leaving. I'll be handing in my resignation tomorrow." I said simply.

"Josie you can't let Dr Cook run you out of the job, we can stand up to him. I'll help you! Nick will help you!" She pleaded. I laughed bitterly and she was taken aback, her fingers fiddling with the hem of her scarf. She sank into Talia's chair. "What am I missing?"

"Nick was heard telling Cook that I'm incapable," I spat. "That and his ongoing seduction game he's been playing."

"Pardon? Seduction?" Her brow furrowed and her mouth hung open.

"Yes. Yes. Dr Nicholas Reeve has had little old me fall completely and utterly head over heels for him." I raised my voice in anger and desperation. "Rachel, I've fallen hook, line and sinker for him and his advances. I *kissed* him. I *kissed* a married man! And not only that, but he's also my boss and apparently, he was just after someone easy. James-the-liar-Cook told me what he's like." There was a pause while Rachel processed what I had said. I leaned forward and put my head into my hands, feeling my bracelet dig into my cheek.

"Nick….and you?" She repeated and I nodded between my fingers. "Wow. Have you…?"

"No. I realised he was married and stopped anything happening."
I mourned. "Rachel, I thought I loved him."

"But…he isn't married, Josie." She said.

"Wh…what?" I paused.

"He was…but not anymore." She sighed. "This is a big thing…if he
likes you. His wife Sienna, she was a GP here too."

"Sienna?" I was bubbling with questions. *Not married?*

"Yes, she was much loved here. She is the mother of his daughters
– he has two girls." I nodded. She continued, "She died."

I sucked in a breath, "What! When?"

"Car accident, three years ago. It was dreadful. He was left with
the girls." She shook her head sadly. "I've not heard of him with a woman
since."

"I…" I suddenly thought of his face when I had mentioned his
wife, and my heart shattered when I recalled what I had said. *'I don't think
your wife would want you messing with one of your staff, do you?'* His
expression, his anger, the way he had stalked away. It all made sense
now, and I sagged heavily. Rachel observed me, waiting.

"He's been trying to help you, you know." She said eventually, when I couldn't find words to speak. "He was…concerned. He wanted to make sure that you were ok."

"James said he told Dr Cook things…" I said slowly.

"It makes no sense… he wanted to help you." She said, chewing her lip.

"None of this adds up. I don't understand. Why doesn't Nick like James?" I asked her.

"I have no idea." She shrugged. "It's time we left…but don't do anything rash. Promise me? We will figure it out tomorrow."

Chapter TWENTY-ONE

Nick

Of all the complete and utter mess-ups that I had made in my life, this had to be up there with one of the worst. Josie, bloody Josie. Sexy, funny, irritatingly stubborn, and sweet Josie. Oh, I had fought not to feel things, convinced that the last of my romantic feelings had gone with Sienna to the grave. And every day since she had gone had been torment, until this undeniably pesky woman had thrown her middle finger into my life and stomped all over a heart I had long presumed calcified.

Josie was everything that Sienna had not been. Her fiery disposition and emotional outbursts opposed the benign nature that my wife once had; we had never argued but the passion had never been quite so... intense. For three years I'd sat in this office, seeing patient after patient after patient, resigned to the banality of my days with the family we had dreamed of together, but without her it had felt empty, and I had found only meaning in the moments I stole with the girls when I managed to get time with them away from my parents.

I was ashamed of how I had broken apart when the accident happened, forgetting that my daughters needed me, and crumbling in the space that she left behind. I had seen countless patients go through this, listened to their weeping monologues or silent disbelief, but never could I have imagined the pain, so visceral in its sensation, and so consuming in its entity.

And that was until I found them. The text messages on her phone that had been handed to me in a cellophane bag of her belongings would haunt me, though I had smashed it on the driveway in anger shortly after. To discover that she had betrayed me while I mourned her absence, was a twisted barb turned slowly. He had stolen her affections and I had already lost her before she was really gone; my opportunity to ask her 'why?' had vanished, and my sadness replaced with a smorgasbord of feelings that were served with simmering anger towards him. The colleague that I had to return to work with after burying my wife, knowing that he was the last person who held her before she was ripped away from my daughters and me.

But I had not spoken of his indiscretion at work, unwilling to taint her memory with idle gossip and shame that our daughters could learn of. I had not given him the satisfaction of being allowed to mourn her openly, and instead I had watched him silently, sick in my enjoyment of his pain and surprisingly angry when he replaced her with a string of in-house scandalous affairs. *He didn't deserve her.*

But James would not do that to Josie. *My Josie.* For she was mine, and I knew that I could not possibly let her get away; I felt a ripple of possessiveness and squeezed my fists. I grunted to myself as I stared at the appointments list on my screen, the clocks appearing next to patient names showing the waiting room was filling up. James was his father's double, and I was amazed that she had not made the connection before now. And Cook had overstayed his welcome in this practice. The complaints were racking up from staff and patients alike, and although I had been respectful to him with his wealth of experience, I had never liked the man. He was sexist. He was misogynistic. He hated seeing a woman in a senior role. He had only tolerated Sienna because she was my wife.

When Rachel had knocked on my door as Josie had left for the day, I had almost launched my chair through the window in anger when I learned how he was treating my girl. I had failed to protect my wife from the father-son duo, but I would not let them put out Josie's fire. My hands had gripped the desk tightly when Rachel told of Josie's tears, her fear of work and concerns that she might leave. It had taken every ounce of self-restraint I possessed not to storm out of my office and into Cook's consulting room three doors down and confront him. But I had not used my fists in years, preferring instead to plan and plot a way to get him out. I held more weight on the board than he, I just needed to figure out what to do.

Outing James as his father's son to Josie had been a good move executed badly. I tapped at my desk with a pen and frowned as I replayed Josie's reaction to the news; it hadn't gone in my favour at all. And while she was angry at me, I felt safe in the knowledge that she would not trust him again. Hardly something to celebrate though when I'd clearly pushed her away. But I had one over on Cook now though. With Josie's statement on top of his dirty history, I could oust him.

The screen flickered; yet another patient had arrived to see me, and I was more than thirty minutes behind my schedule. I sighed and opened the next patient record on the list. It was going to be a long afternoon.

Chapter TWENTY-TWO

Josie

By the time I reached my car and threw in my bag, the rain was aggressively bouncing on the ground. I slammed the car door shut after climbing in, and started the engine, pulling out of the car park with my damp hair dripping a little down my neck and causing me to shiver. I drummed my fingers on the steering wheel, my thoughts drifting to Nick. He wasn't married... but his backstory was utterly tragic, and my heart squeezed for those beautiful girls of his who had lost their mother.

I pulled onto the main road and turned up the radio to attempt to drown out the argument raging inside my head. Torn between joy at his single status, rage at his comments to Cook, and heartache for his pain in his loss, I couldn't settle myself at all. I had so many questions and so much to feel. *And James.* How COULD he withhold that Cook was his father? I knew I'd be calling Rosie to brain-dump when I got home.

The rain battered the car and the lights of other vehicles blurred against my windscreen as the darkness fell on the journey home. The combination of the dark and rain made for my own personal worst set of driving conditions, and I grimaced. There was a sudden vibration in the steering and a banging sound, the car clunking more than usual and the smooth ride now stuttering and jerking me about. I couldn't keep driving like this, especially since one side of the car felt to be dragging.

"Oh Terry…" I muttered to myself, and indicated to pull over, squinting in the mirror through the glare of car headlights in the rain to check it was safe to pull into the side of the road; I threw on my hazard lights. Pushing the door open against the wind was my first challenge, the rain soaking straight through my jacket and my shirt within seconds of exposure, the cold spreading straight to my skin. "Ugh!"

I hurried around to the back of the car, covering my face in a half-hearted attempt to protect it from the downfall. The flat tyre was immediately obvious, and I yelled in frustration, my already frayed temper giving way to a bubble of rage.

"No! Why? NO!" I kicked the wheel and slammed my hands onto the side of the car, wincing as the pain spread up my foot and my hands began to smart, the water seeping through the soles in my pumps. "Could this day get any worse!"

I began to sob, my tears only a drop in the deluge of rain, my hands grabbing at my hair in despair and a roar of pent-up anger burst out, unheard in the pounding of the rain in the dark. *Come on. Get it together Josie.* Through the sobs, I yanked open the car boot and began fumbling for my kit, pulling up the spare wheel cover to look for the jack.

Keep going. I set it up, my fingers slipping on the cold metal, and pushed it under the side of the car next to the deflated tyre. A puddle had gathered at the roadside and my fingers shook while I screwed in the handle. I had never done this before, but my dad had shown me how years ago. I grimaced as my feet squelched inside my shoes in the puddle and prepared myself to start pumping up the side of the car.

"WHY did I wear a bloody skirt!" I yelled to nobody as I dragged my sodden skirt up my legs just enough so that I could bend to start jacking up the car. I groaned with every pump, feeling any remaining warmth in me replaced by the spread of a painful, cold, and icy feeling. I steadied myself for a moment by grabbing the roof of the car and sagged into the door, contemplating defeat.

"JOSIE, WHAT ARE YOU DOING?" I turned and threw up my arms to shield my eyes, blinded by headlights from a car that I'd not heard pull up behind me.

"Who?" Parting my fingers enough to squint through them, I could see a tall, male figure approaching. He staggered in the wind; his arm thrown above his head to protect his face. When he lined up in front of me, the shadow cast between us let me see his familiar blonde hair and

I instinctively turned away to restart jacking the car. I wasn't ready to see him yet.

"Josie!" Nick yelled. "This is ridiculous, I'll take you home! We can sort it tomorrow." He grabbed my arm, but I shrugged him off.

"Leave me alone!" I yelled above the wind.

"I can help you! Let me help!"

"NO! Funnily enough, I CAN do things independently." I screamed out, the blustering of the wind and rain topped with sudden thunder making it hard to make myself heard. My underwear was soaked now, and I could feel my clothes clinging to me. I was so desperate to get home and peel them off.

"Why won't you let me help you?" He shouted.

"Why did you tell Cook I was incapable?" I threw back, abandoning the jack handle and turning to him, his hair and face as soaked as mine now, water dripping off the end of his nose.

"What? I didn't!"

"James said you did! Don't lie to me! I know about your wife. I know about it all!" There was a flash in the sky behind me, and it lit his stricken face for a fraction of a second. I counted to four and thunder rumbled overhead.

"I didn't say that at all! Will you come and get in my car, and I can explain?!" He reached out for my shoulder, but I yanked it free.

"Don't TOUCH me. I thought I could trust you!" I started shaking, the cold seeming to seep into my bones.

"JOSIE. Listen, James will say anything...ANYTHING to get at me. He's a lying bastard. I told Dr Cook that you needed clinical support, not that you're incapable! I'm trying to help you!" He pulled off his coat and pulled it round my shoulders, pushing my protesting arms away.

"But why-" Another flash and I could see his hair was slick to his forehead, I counted one....two. The lightening was getting closer to us.

"He slept with her...my wife...before the accident." He dropped his head as I gasped.

"What!" The lightening flashed again, and it was close.

"Your keys, give me your keys! In the car, now!" He pulled me away from my car, grabbing my keys from my hand. "Go get in my car!"

I hesitated, watching him rush to lower the jack, but he caught me staring and shouted again, "GO!"

I rushed to climb into the passenger seat of the Lexus as he pushed the jack into the boot of my car, grabbed my bag from the passenger side and locked it, running against the rain back to the car. He climbed in, breathless, as another bolt of lightning struck on the road ahead.

"I'll take you home and we can sort your car tomorrow." He panted, clipping his seatbelt on, and pushing a button inside the car.

"Nick I-"

"Forget about it. Nobody else knows what happened and I didn't know until after the accident anyway. He manipulates people." There was a hint of weariness in his voice that I hadn't heard before.

"That must have been awful, I'm so sorry." There was a silence in the car as he pulled away into the rain, leaving my car behind. "I'm sorry for everything. For thinking you were married too-"

"Josie, you don't need to apologise." He said firmly. "I haven't been upfront at all." My teeth chattered, and he turned on the heated seating which warmed me to some degree, but with clothes that needed wringing out, it made little difference. "Are you two... is something going on?"

"Me and James? Hell no." The rain lashed the windscreen as we approached my house. "Are you coming in? To... to get warm? I can dry your clothes?"

He stole a look at me when the car stopped on my drive, "Sure. The girls are at my parents."

I flicked on the light as we stumbled into the hallway, embarrassed at the number of shoes littering the floor by the door. "Sorry about the mess. Come in." I was grateful that I'd timed the heating on, and I kicked off the squidgy pumps while peeling off his coat that I still wore, and then my jacket. I sank into the radiator and sighed as I felt heat warm my bare legs, the skirt damp and uncomfortable.

He kicked off his shoes and began unbuttoning the white shirt he wore; it was soaked through, clinging to him in a way that did nothing to deceive me of what lay underneath, his chest hair pasted flat to his taught skin. He caught me sneaking a look, the side of his mouth curling up into a bemused smile, and I flushed.

"Josie… you're staring."

"You're all wet…"

"So are you." He smirked, "Do you need a hand?" And without waiting for me to answer, he pulled open his shirt, before coming to me at the radiator and beginning to undo each of the delicate buttons on my top, exposing more of me as his fingers lowered with each opening.

Goosebumps erupted on my arms as he pulled the last of the silk top out of my skirt, and dragged it over my shoulders, letting it float to the floor.

He traced his fingers down my neck, pushing the wet hair out of the way, and leaned in, hungrily mouthing my neck and I sighed, moving my head to give up more of me for him to kiss. His arms pulled at my waist, and I closed my eyes, savouring the roughness of his chin against my ear, the warmth of his chest against my sticky skin.

His shirt had to go, and I tugged it down his arms, fighting the strain of his muscle and draping my arms around his neck once he was free. The kisses to my body grew in intensity and as his mouth finally met mine, devouring it, I raked my nails through his hair, left gasping when he pulled away.

"Nothing is stopping me now." He breathed.

"Is this what you want?" I asked.

"I want you." He growled darkly. For just a second, I paused, taking in the sight of us, soaking wet and half dressed, he in his trousers and me in my bra and skirt in the hallway. I began to giggle, and he frowned, "What's so funny?"

"This! We're in my hallway like drowned rats!" I laughed harder when I caught sight of Astrophe in the kitchen doorway looking about as suspicious as a cat could possibly look. "I can't have sex in the hallway!"

"Who says it ends here?" He laughed, the hint of mischief in his eye.

"But the cat!" There were tears in my eyes from giggling so hard.

"It's a cat."

"She can't watch her mama do the nasty!" He shook his head in disbelief, looking between me and the cat and then I squealed when I realised what he planned to do, the second before he scooped me up with his arms and threw me over his shoulder, slapping my butt.

"Lead the way then... where's a cat-free zone?" And I giggled more as he carried me through the house to my bedroom, shutting us inside and throwing me onto the bed.

"That skirt has to come off."

"Do away with the trousers then soldier." I pulled off my skirt and waited by the pillows in my underwear, watching as he removed the remainder of his clothes and giving him an approving smirk as his belt clanged on the floor at the foot of the bed.

"You know Toyota, you're a little *too* cocky." He brushed his hair off his face.

"At least I'm not a dick…" I said, my eyes dropping as I bit my lip.

"Well, I'm certainly going to give you one of those." He crawled up the bed as I giggled again, before he stopped me abruptly with a rough kiss, unhooking the lace bra and discarding it to the floor. "I've been wanting to do this since the day you gave me the finger."

"Shh now," I put a finger across his lips and dropped my voice to mock his, "This *'requires concentration'*." He groaned, and lowered his body to mine, only a thin stretch of lace remaining between our skin. A ripple of excitement pooled between my legs, and I reached up to cup his face.

"Don't mess with me Toyota." He warned.

"Or *what,* Lexus?" I challenged, wiggling my hips into him with a triumphant smile. He grabbed my hands suddenly, and pinned them above my head, his eyes heavy with desire and his jaw set. There was a frisson of electricity where our bodies met, sparks cascading down my thighs and I arched my back to meet him, our chests pressed together. The surprise in his eyes told me he felt it too, but he held my arms firmly in place as he found ways to tease me with his mouth, taunt me with flashes of pleasure that left my legs trembling with anticipation and my toes curling against the bedcovers.

"Nick…" I pleaded at last, but he did not respond with words, using one hand to peel off the last remaining soaked piece of clothing between us. And with nothing holding him back, he nudged open my knees and took exactly what I'd been waiting to give him all along. His hips slammed into me, and I cried out in ecstasy with each collision, my hands still trapped, but my legs free to pull him in deeper, and deeper.

I moaned with each stroke, my fingernails digging into my own palms so hard that I was certain to have left a mark. I wanted him, *all of him,* and for this frenzy to continue evermore, until we were both spent.

"Nick…" I panted. He grunted in response. "Nick!" I urged him. His eyes snapped to mine as I felt myself beginning to climax, determined to see the look in his eyes as it happened.

"I…love….you." He breathed and our mouths parted in shock just as we were both overcome together.

My heart pounded as he rested himself onto the bed, our legs still intertwined, and he sighed heavily with his eyes closed. *He said he loved me. HE SAID HE LOVED ME. Should I say it back or was it said in the moment? Did I love him too?* And instinctively as soon as I asked myself the question, this bubble of warmth floated up inside and burst, spreading

this indescribable tingly feeling that caused an involuntary wiggle of

delight.

"Toyota?" He murmured; his face planted into the pillow.

"Mmm?"

"I meant what I said, even if you're not ready to say it yet." I

paused, a grin widening across my face, and lifted my head to plant a kiss

on his bare shoulder.

"I think I do though," I whispered. His eyes opened, and he lifted

his head a little to inspect me. "love you...I mean." And when the smile

broke across his face, I basked in the light it brought into his eyes, and

pulled him down, hungry for another kiss.

*   *   *

I awoke to the sound of purring and felt nothing but bliss. Bliss

and aching. Bliss and aching *and* hunger. I cracked open one eye to see

where the purring originated from and almost fell off my bed in shock.

The memories of the night before resurfaced and suddenly the aching in

my legs made sense, as I saw Nick's peaceful sleeping face beside me. I reddened when I thought of what those lips had done and the roughness of his face against intimate skin. I couldn't ever remember having had a night like that before, stopping only when I was too exhausted to continue.

Astrophe lay on his chest purring and catching sight of my open eyes, she stretched out a paw and let it rest on his cheek possessively, serving me with a filthy expression, before resuming her half-lidded watch over his slumber. Oh, he was owned – her taste was impeccable.

I snuck a look at my phone, where there were several missed texts and a call from Rosie. *'If I don't hear from you by 7.30am, I'm sending a search party round.'* It was 7.24am, so I fired off a message, *'I'm ok. Had a flat tyre last night so got a lift home. Said driver is currently asleep in my bed.'* I smiled to myself as I imagined her expression as she read my message. In record time, the phone buzzed within a minute: *'Details. Now. Tea at mine too – Mike is working late.'*

"Good morning." Nick smiled sleepily from the pillow next to me, "Are you going to tell me what I'm supposed to do with him?" He nodded at Astrophe, whose purring had increased in volume.

"Her. You can't leave now until she does. It's an unspoken rule." I gave her a pet on the head. "Did you sleep ok?"

"I did. I was…tired." He shuffled up the bed and Astrophe hopped down next to him, having more tolerance for his jostling than she usually offered me. "What's her name?"

"Astrophe. She's a fan of yours." I grumbled jealously as I sat up while he fussed her.

"As in..cat-astrophe?" He asked, his eyebrows raised in bemusement. I nodded and he chuckled. "You really are something else."

We sat together in silence but for the purring of the cat, and I had a strange temptation to take a photo of him. His tousled bed hair, his jaw cast in shadow from a need to shave, my ancient floral bedding covering his exceedingly delicious thighs, and my batty cat headbutting his cheek from her stance on the pillow, his hand reaching up to tickle her baggy underbelly.

"Penny for them…" He said.

"I was just selfishly hoping that this isn't a one-off." I picked at the frayed edge of the bedding, nervous.

"Well, that would be a catastrophe wouldn't it…" He grinned. "Of course not, I was kind of hoping to take you on a date? If that satisfies the lady and her faithful feline?"

"Of course."

"But first, work. And a flat tyre."

Chapter TWENTY-THREE

Josie

Once Nick had rushed home to change and back, he picked me up in his car to take us to work. The closer we got, the more my seat felt to be claiming me as its own, as I shrank down into it trying to avoid having to leave the safety of his car. I stole a glance over at Nick with his now clean-shaven face and still-damp hair from the shower, and smiled.

"You're staring again." He said and moved his hand to my leg.

"I can't help it." He squeezed my leg gently, and I thought of everything I'd learned about him yesterday. "It was ridiculously kind of you not to tell everyone what James did."

There was silence and I wondered if I had stepped too far. "It wasn't for his benefit." He said, his eyes not leaving the road. "I didn't want her memory overshadowed by the affair. And I don't want my girls to know."

"How did you find out?" I asked tentatively.

"The police gave me her phone after the accident. I have never spoken to him about it, but I made it clear that I am aware, we used to be good friends." He seemed remarkably at ease discussing the topic.

"You are a bigger person than I." I stated simply and he took his eyes off the road for a second to flash me a small smile.

"No. I have had to fight every single urge not to steal you away and have my way with you since you first stepped foot into the practice, even if you were a feisty know-it-all. And even now, all I want to do is turn this car around and take you back to bed." He smirked and his hand squeezed my leg again, before returning to the gearstick. "We are going to be a few minutes late, but don't worry Toyota...I shan't punish you for the indiscretion, at least not straight away."

I sighed quietly when I thought of work. The inevitability of having to face Dr Cook made returning to bed an even more delicious prospect, "Yes please to returning to bed."

"Rachel told me about everything you know. Quite honestly, I count myself lucky you haven't resigned." He said as he pulled onto the road near work.

"Well, you kinda ruined my plans – last night I was heading home to write my letter to say I planned to leave. I was going to ask Rosie to take me back... I might still ask her." I picked at my nails as I remembered Cook's scathing remarks and I felt the anxious tremor begin.

"No." he said firmly. "We will not lose you. *I* will not lose you."

"I can't work like this." He pulled us into his parking space and, seeing that my hands were shaking, put his own hands on to steady them.

"Does this happen often?"

"Every day" I felt silly, ashamed that I had reached this low point over a few measly comments. My eyes smarted and I blinked furiously to stop myself from crying again.

"I had no idea – you should have come to me." There was movement along the front of the car, and I saw Rachel walking past towards the staff entrance. She did a double take, her eyes widening when she saw us in the car together, and her mouth falling open. Nick looked up and saw her frozen by the door and she quickly rushed inside.

"She's going to demand to know why I'm sat in your car." I sniffed.

"And what are you going to say?"

"That you kidnapped me in a storm, stole my cat's affections, and insisted on returning me to work despite heavy protestations." He laughed and yet it was time to go inside. At the foot of the stairs, he grabbed my hand and kissed it lightly.

"Let me sort this out." he said.

"No. Please. I'm going to speak to Anne today. And before you say anything, I know she will come to you anyway, but I have to be the one to say something first. I don't want special treatment." He nodded reluctantly and I left him watching me climb the staircase. I turned and winked from the top, and the worry in his mouth spread into a lopsided grin; an expression I recognised as reserved just for me. I was marginally tempted to run after him, because up the stairs and along the corridor suddenly felt too far away.

The novelty of his affections was not lost on me, and I had to resist a delighted wiggle as I made my way down the upstairs corridor to the pharmacy office, my red face a signalling beacon declaring, *'New love! New love!'*. *Is it love?* I pushed the thought aside as the office door came into view and the chatter of voices could be heard through the wood.

The door opened to a chorus of 'good morning!' but Rachel looked like she was painstakingly holding in questions, and I laughed as I watched her fight the urge to stand up and begin cross-examination.

"Morning Rachel..." I said shyly as I seated myself down with a smile.

"Don't you 'Morning-Rachel' me!" She hissed under her breath. "You owe me answers....stat! You can start by telling me why you appeared in Nick Reeve's car this morning and your car was nowhere to be seen…."

She was not one to mince her words at all and I stifled a chuckle, glancing around to see Talia on the phone, and Tina concentrating on a discharge. "My car broke down…he gave me a lift."

She paused to think, before launching phase two of questioning. "So, what happened to hating his guts yesterday? Why did you both look guilty? And why, in god's name…was he holding your hands?!" Her head trembled with every question, her short hair swishing in her giddiness to drag out more information.

"My car broke down last night on my way home and he happened to be driving past." I whispered quickly. "He rescued me in the storm and drove me home, while also explaining some things that made sense…and declaring his feelings for me."

Her eyes widened and she found herself suddenly mute. "Oy, Rachel… have you seen a ghost?" Tina called and she shook her head.

"What in the muttering is going on?" Talia asked as she hung up the phone.

"My car broke down last night in the storm and I had to get a lift in today... I was worried I might get in trouble for being late." *Well, it wasn't a lie.*

"Oh, do you need a lift home?" Tina asked, hanging up her own call and I shook my head in gratitude.

"So..." Rachel managed.

"So, I guess we might be going on a date soon." I grinned and she fist-pumped the air and quickly dropped her hand in case the others saw, and we silently giggled between ourselves at the table, Talia throwing us a bemused look as she answered another call.

The morning tasks distracted me well enough, but I knew that I had to be true to my word to Nick and speak to Anne about what had gone on between Dr Cook and I. I felt truly silly and terribly frightened. It wasn't a fear of losing my job per se, but more a fear that my reputation would be damaged and that these ladies who I sat with, who I had come to consider friends, would see me differently. I was worried that in making a complaint, or raising a concern, it would make me more vulnerable, and it would open speculation that Dr Cook's perception of my inadequacy was the correct judgement of me. If he had reason to think that I was not good enough, then perhaps others would too, and when his concerns were given voice, then it might become consensus. I shuddered at the thought, trying to tell myself that it mattered not what others thought of me, only that I knew I was doing my very best.

But this fear had become toxic. It had taken over my life inside and outside work and eaten into my relationships with friends and colleagues. It had darkened my days and left me feeling weak and worthless. Small comments had made me feel smaller and isolated, and I had been fighting inferiority with futile attempts, taking one man's disdain, and using every opportunity to devalue myself, one day at a time. But I was not worthless, and I was sad that it had taken Nick to show me that.

'She remembered who she was, and the game changed' The Lalah Deliah quote from Nick's text, and the book on my bookshelf, crept into my mind and I gasped, feeling a reserve of something...something like grit and a sprinkling of my old confidence scattering in the pit of my gut.

"Earth to Josie..." Tina said, "Are you ok?"

"I will be... but I've not been. I've not been ok for a while now. I must do something... I'll be back." And with that, I convinced myself to go downstairs and knock on Anne's door. My body was trembling so much that I felt unsteady, bile rose in my throat and my heart raced so much that I felt breathless. But it was time to take control and confront my fears.

"Is everything OK Josie?" She asked as she examined me over the top of her glasses.

"I think... I think I need to discuss something with you."

Chapter TWENTY-FOUR

Nick

"She's raised a damned complaint about me, Reeve." His voice followed the bang as my door swung open, and Giles Cook himself strutted into my consulting room, where I had been sitting, poring over blood results. *Ugh*. I felt my mood sink instantly, knowing that this was a conversation I had not particularly looked forward to. I knew what I had to do.

"She has."

"She – wait." He sank onto the bed, frowning over his spectacles. "You knew?" I paused for a moment, releasing the mouse from my grip, and stood to push the door back into its frame. This wasn't a conversation that I wanted to be overheard.

"I did." I turned back to my chair and sank into it, this time facing him. Age had not served him well and if it wasn't for his historically atrocious behaviour towards the women in this practice, I might have felt sorry for him.

"And you did not discourage her?" He snapped, as was his custom.

"I did not." There was a silence, in which his piggy little eyes darted about the room. He was my senior by at least twenty years, though I had never found him passionate about patient care and it disappointed me to hear many of our patients express their disdain for his attitude. "In fact, Giles, she came to me for advice, and I encouraged her."

"You did what?" He froze, a dark undertone to his voice. He was a broad man, and I could see why so many of my female colleagues had found him intimidating. I recalled Josie's fear-filled eyes and trembling hands and had to force myself not to visibly recoil from him in disgust. He was everything I despised in a man, and worse that he was colleague in healthcare.

"I listened to her experiences and found that the behaviour she had experienced from you was neither professional nor appropriate. I encouraged her to follow the appropriate channels in reporting this." I said quietly. The tension in the room was entirely palpable.

"I taught you everything you know." He said slowly and maliciously, making no attempt to defend himself.

"No. I didn't learn respect from you because in that Giles you are sorely lacking. She is not the first to make a complaint as you well know, and I have been slow to act on the complaints, blinded by the years I spent as your trainee."

He stood suddenly and I did the same in response, "Who do you th-"

"You would do well to watch what you say, Giles." I raised my voice a degree, feeling my hands ball into fists that I knew I would not use. "The complaint will go through the process and be fed to the board, and Josie will be seeking legal advice. Your *large* file of complaints will not work in your favour, and I will be making sure it is available for thorough examination, along with access to statements from various staff that have left on your account. That is, unless you suddenly find yourself craving an earlier than planned retirement. You will not harass and belittle my staff anymore, Giles. How you choose to leave, is in your hands." I raised my eyebrows at him, his eyes had dropped to his feet, a red flush of anger in his face.

I turned to pick up my empty mug, sorely in need of a coffee and suddenly itching to visit Josie where I knew she sat upstairs. I glanced back at where he remained mute and stiff, "You have twenty-four hours."

I only became aware of my pulse pounding as I yanked open the door and set off up the corridor to the kitchenette. I could only hope that he would not fight against this, nor call my bluff on the legal action I had lied about. Josie would likely kill me if she heard what I had told him, for I was sure she had no intentions of seeking legal advice. I contemplated if I could possibly convince her, even if I paid the legal fees myself.

"Are you going to tell me why I've just seen Giles almost run over one of our patients in haste to leave the carpark?" Anne's voice carried down the corridor as I hunted for the milk.

"Excellent." I said with my head in the fridge, smirking to myself. "He will be leaving us soon. Prepare an advert for a full-time position. As soon as he has resigned, we can go live."

Her mouth was open when I resurfaced with the milk. "What have you done?" She whispered.

"What should have been done a long time ago. Don't worry, I'll redistribute the remains of his clinic between us."

*   *   *

"Tell me what's happening then." Josie buttoned up her jacket as we prepared to leave. The cold outside was bitter, and regardless of the heated seats of the car, I had warned her that I almost froze in my earlier home visits. Two days had passed since Giles had left the building after our brief discussion and he had communicated only in email, stated sickness as a reason for absence, and just this morning we had received notification that he intended to leave and step back as a partner. The information was sensitive until the next partner meeting.

"Nuh-huh. You know I can't." She pouted in response, and I felt a flash of delight coarse through me. "I do require something from you though." She raised her eyebrows, stuffing her hands into her pockets as I pushed my arms into the sleeves of my own coat. "Just a small thing."

I took two steps towards her and quickly posted my arms through hers, pulling her into me by her waist, inhaling the sweet smell of her perfume and nudging her nose with my own. "A kiss?"

"Only if you tell me what is going on." She huffed.

"Thursday." I hadn't realised just how much working at the practice under Giles Cook had affected her, until I felt her shaking hands every morning as she entered the building, despite safe in the knowledge that he would no longer be working with her.

"Okay. But he isn't the only one that needs to change though Nick." She sighed. "The culture he's fostered here isn't right."

"I know and I need your help with that too…all of the team. Will you?" I asked her earnestly. She paused as she thought, glancing at her feet as her hair fell forward.

"Yes, I think I have an idea."

Chapter TWENTY-FIVE

Josie

"It's going to be fine." Nick wrapped his arms around me in his room and kissed the top of my head, as we prepared to head to a meeting with the partners.

"You promise?" I looked up at him.

"Yes. They agreed to the meeting didn't they..." He said, adding in an undertone, "not that I'd have given them a choice."

The meeting started in a few minutes, and I thought back to Anne's reaction the previous week when I had told her everything. I had described in detail how I had been treated, the profound impact it had had on my life, and how I felt that things could be improved for the pharmacy team in a way that was respectful and encouraging for each individual team member. Anne had been shocked and horrified, and I had struggled to speak through my tears, suggesting that I could not continue in this role if I was going to have to deal with being treated like this.

As Nick had predicted, Anne approached him following my confession and Nick assured me that he had been especially frank with Dr Cook, painting the reality of his behaviour harshly and demanding a whole team meeting with the partners and the pharmacy staff.

When I had confessed my experience to the team, they had rallied around me and even admitted to feeling intimidated themselves. Talia had embraced me with tears in her eyes and said that she too had felt frightened to ask questions.

It soon became clear, after Nick confirmed rumours, that Dr Cook had taken his leave and resigned. I didn't know the ins and outs, though I suspected Nick might have had a hand in that and it wasn't entirely down to my complaint. But the fact remained that I would never be the same person again, having lost confidence and gained a whole lot of anxiety. The shaking of my fingers, thumping of my heart, nightmares and cold sweats had built themselves into my daily routine and I was struggling to overcome the grasp it had over me, even knowing that he was gone.

"You're stronger than you know." Nick said.

"I know what I have to do." I said, putting my head against his chest once more, "Then I can focus on the important things."

"Which are?" His lips moved against the top of my head.

"You... Us. " I felt him smile.

The training room had been fashioned into a conference-style set up, small tables nestled together to form one long, large one that was intimidating. The partners sat along one side, Nick taking a space in the middle next to Dr Ambrose, and the girls filed in around me as I took a seat in the middle of the opposite side. Rachel sat on one side of me, Talia squeezing my leg under the table to my right.

There was a sprinkle of conversation across the table for a few moments and sweat gathered in my shaky palms; I tapped my foot nervously and chewed the inside of my lip. I'd spent a week preparing for this meeting with the girls, using Rosie as a sounding board in the evenings when Nick had been busy at home with his girls, and I had been left with a sulking Astrophe, clearly missing her male caller. But it was time to stand up for myself, and my team too.

A hush settled in the room as Anne appeared and sat at the head of the table, and I received two further leg squeezes, and an encouraging nod from Nick across the table.

"Hi everybody and thank you for attending, especially as it was short notice. As some of you are aware, our pharmacy team have a presentation they want to make to the partnership. Josie, I think you are speaking first? Good. Go ahead."

"Th…thank you." I stood, but the cue card I held shook with my fingers, and I hastily put it back on the table. "And thank you all for attending today. I started at this practice earlier this year as a new pharmacy technician and I was full of excitement, and wonder. I had fresh ideas and I was determined to demonstrate that my skills as a pharmacy technician were valuable, invaluable in fact. I wanted to learn. I wanted to soak up information from you all like a sponge, so that I could go on to use my skills to benefit you as well as our patients.

But it became apparent very quickly that my need to learn was not a priority, and I began to feel the weight of unnecessary expectation. I could not learn everything without your guidance and yet I could not know enough for you, be enough for you or do enough for these patients." I looked at each GP in turn, some had the courtesy to look down in shame.

"My colleagues and I have a wealth of experience, these ladies more than I in general practice. But our skills are not your skills and nor do we ever expect them to be. This does not mean that our skills are any less worthwhile and need any less opportunity for development." I caught Nick's eyes and faltered for a second, but he smiled encouragingly. I took a deep breath, glancing at each of the seven partners in turn.

"In the last month, we have turned around the management of hypertension in this practice. We've trained staff in appropriate recording of data, worked with community pharmacies, identified patients overmedicated, under-medicated and not medicated at all. We've improved the immediate quality of life of some patients and reduced the risk of many others. These ladies –" I looked to Talia and to Tina, "have single-handedly organised clinics and home visits, liaising with pharmacies to provide more community access to patients."

"And Holly –" I glanced to where she sat, smiling shyly, "She's prescribed and deprescribed so many drugs for these patients, alongside her usual work, to get this project off the ground."

"Rachel here –" I looked down to my side where she nodded, clearly emotional, "Has taught me more about being a practice technician than I could give her credit for. She's helped teach me how to monitor patients and navigate my way around the record. She gave me confidence when I had none."

Every single partner had their eyes on me. I felt bolstered by their careful attention, and I stood tall. *So, this is what speech-giving felt like.* "I became a pharmacy technician because I wanted to be more and do more for patients. This small team of women sitting next to me have made a huge difference to one patient cohort in just one month. We make a huge difference to the whole patient population every day. As a newcomer, I have felt the fear of asking for help. I have felt cast aside and I worry that my fears will one day overshadow the passion I have for pharmacy. We spend so much time justifying our work and our worth to patients and I ask you all, please don't make us feel like we must justify ourselves to you too. I want to come to work and feel empowered and supported and fulfilled. They do too." I gestured to the team sat around me. I paused to draw breath and Holly stood to speak, as we had planned.

"As the pharmacist on the team, I'm duty bound to speak too, and I hope to do so as candidly as Josie." I sat back and listened intently to everything she said, about the dedication of the team, the multitude of projects we all wanted to undertake, the training we all had, and the collective feeling of being undervalued and unsupported. She spoke with an air of authority that I didn't feel I had been able to muster, commanding respect in stature and in spoken word. Rachel grabbed my hand, which I had placed on my leg to stop it shaking, and I gave her a slight smile. Holly finished and sat down.

"I think it's clear the impact the team have had and even more so now, with Josie's introduction." Anne spoke again. "As practice manager, I have huge respect for the work you all do, and I know our admin staff couldn't do without you all."

"If you don't mind me adding just one thing, Anne." She nodded at me and I continued, "This presentation isn't about us trying to stand above any person or any team. The aim of our approach today, is to share our experience of feeling unsupported and to ask respectfully, for that support and kindness. Working in general practice has been a huge eyeopener for me, and I see and feel the pressure we all carry to keep the train going, the patients using us as they need. But unless each team member is treated with equal value and respect, then people will struggle to maintain passion, and the patients won't benefit. And ultimately, isn't the whole point of this place..." I gestured around, "to provide care?"

I sat down heavily, my work done, and my team looking nervous. Nick said, "Thank you. All of you. I'd appreciate some time here to discuss things and then I shall come up and see you all later this afternoon." He nodded at me as we rose to leave, and I couldn't even muster a return gesture. We filed out of the training room one-by-one in silence.

"We've made an awful mistake." I said eventually as we reached the pharmacy office. "What if they consider it disrespectful that we've come forward and said we aren't supported enough? What if you all lose your jobs because of my hare-brained scheme?" I started to panic, suddenly losing breath again.

"Hey!" Talia grabbed my shoulders, "We aren't getting fired. They need us. What happened in there today needed to happen. We stood up for ourselves and we asked for what we deserve: respect and support."

"She's right, Josie. We kicked ass. You kicked ass." Tina wriggled with a tired smile.

"I'm so proud of you." Rachel muscled in and enveloped me in a hug.

"We all are." Holly said from her desk. The team returned to their work around me, and I restarted my computer to attempt to get on with more work, a list of patients as long as I'd ever seen it in the pharmacy inbox. I don't think any of us could concentrate all that well; even Holly didn't seem to be getting through her inbox as quickly as she would normally. As the afternoon wore on, the tension grew while we waited for Nick's feedback from the partner discussion. On more than one occasion I saw the others' eyes flick to the clock on the wall, my own glancing at the on-screen time.

Eventually I grew tired of waiting and decided to go make more coffees, carrying a tray downstairs to the kitchenette.

"Josie, can we talk?" James had joined me.

"What's up James?" I sighed as I prepared the drinks.

"You've been avoiding me... I just want to check that you're ok."
He put his hand on my arm to stop me reaching for another cup.

"Look, I know you can't be found guilty by association with your
father, but you've not exactly been honest about who you are – and
you've lied to me about others." I shrugged his hand away and turned to
him. "Nick might be able to move on, but I certainly can't. I don't hand out
second chances anymore."

His shoulders sagged, his eyes shifting to his feet. "We all make
mistakes Josie." I felt my resolve flicker but remembering the hurt in
Nick's face when he told me what James had done was enough not to
weaken.

"Making mistakes is one thing James, but you lied to me about
Nick. I'm done." I turned back to the cups and left him to walk away. It
was the right thing to do, and I pushed aside a smidge of sadness. I
returned upstairs to where the ladies were working and passed around
the mugs, fighting the shaky hands not to spill their drinks.

"Ladies, I'm being honest here but I'm not sure I'm ever going to
recover from all of this. I feel constantly on the edge of danger,
sometimes without even realising what I'm worrying about." I sagged into
my chair.

"You will Josie. You've got us and time...lots of time." Rachel soothed. Nick's head suddenly appeared around our door, making us all jump.

"Well, that's a first ladies." He smiled at us all, "You certainly caused some disagreements among the partners."

"So, are we fired, or what?" Tina said to break the tension, and there was a ripple of laughter.

"Certainly not. But we've agreed there needs to be more support for you as a team and individually, including pharmacy specific meetings, regular one-to-ones, and drop-in sessions. In the end it was a unanimous decision, and I will be developing plans with you all next week. We're going to help you be as great as I know you can be. Well done, ladies."

"YES!" Tina jumped and Talia wiped her eyes. Holly clapped her hands together in delight and Rachel pulled me into a bear hug. Nick slipped out with a wink to me before the door closed.

"Anyone for the pub tonight?" Tina demanded.

"It's a school night!" Rachel said.

"eff it Friday then..."

"So... Jos, rumours are a-mongering." Tina sidled up to me, a cheeky twinkle in her eye. "Rumours involving you."

"They…they are?" My eyes widened and I glanced to Rachel who snickered and shook her head. Holly paused from packing her bag, Talia froze with her hand on the telephone receiver. "And what have I done?"

"It isn't a case of what you've done exactly." Talia giggled as Tina leaned down and peered over her glasses in mock-examination of me, "Its who." Rachel guffawed and Holly gasped.

"Pardon?" I reddened and bit my lip in a terrible attempt to stem a giggle myself.

"Have you, or have you not been fraternising with a colleague?" She demanded with a grin.

"Getting cosy in a consultation room?" Talia piped up.

"Examining each other in the early hours?" Rachel joined the fray.

"Getting dirty with the doctor in the house?" Holly chimed in and there was a collective gasp, and everyone's heads swivelled in her direction in shock. She laughed heartily, and looked at me, waiting, "Well?"

"A lady doesn't kiss and tell." I said eventually.

"Good job you aren't a bloody lady then, eh Josie?" Tina punched me lightly on the arm, and I surrendered happily to interrogation until half past five on the clock signalled the end of the day.

"Looks like it's a lift in the Lexus for you again, Toyota." Nick said as he opened the carpark door after we finished work. "Time to ditch Terry?"

"Never!"

"Do you think…do you think you'd like to come and meet the girls officially this weekend?" He asked as he opened the passenger door for me.

"Of course, but what exactly are we going to tell them is going on between us?" I leaned against the car.

"Us? This?" He put his hand on the roof next to my head and his gaze fell onto me, a slow and sexy smile pulling a dimple into his cheek, "It's real…actual, love, isn't it?"

And I pulled him closer by the length of his tie and whispered into his ear, with my lips grazing against his skin, grinning as I said, "I guess you could say it is, technically speaking".

Thank you so much for taking the time to read Love, Technically

Speaking. I hope you enjoyed the story. Sadly, lots of people experience

bullying in the workplace and don't have such a positive ending. If you find

yourself struggling in the workplace, please seek help...you are not alone.

For Pharmacists in the UK, Pharmacist Support charity provides help,

advice, and access to resources. For my UK readers, please consider

reaching out to the MIND charity if you are struggling with mental health,

regardless of trigger.

For my international readers, do not suffer in silence and look at

local resources available to you, talk to a friend, family, or trusted

colleague.

Do not accept being treated any less than you deserve.

All my love,

Laura

Printed in Great Britain
by Amazon